992824829 X

FORBIDDEN

Sue is trying to forget a broken love-affair when she meets Ross Bryant. Handsome and successful, he is everything any woman could want — but Sue isn't just any woman. Although she allows Ross to make love to her, her whole being is still wrapped-up in the tortured affair with the married Paul. Bewildered and shattered, Sue contemplates the two men in her life — the darkly-handsome Ross, the debonair Paul who desperately wants her back. But how does a woman choose, or reject? How can she settle for a love less true and passionate than the one she knew?

Books by Patricia Robins
Published by The House of Ulverscroft:

FORSAKEN
FOREVER

PATRICIA ROBINS

◆

FORBIDDEN

Complete and Unabridged

ULVERSCROFT
Leicester

First published in Great Britain in 1992

First Large Print Edition
published 2000

British Library CIP Data

Robins, Patricia, *1921 –*
Forbidden.—Large print ed.—
Ulverscroft large print series: romance
1. Love stories
2. Large type books
I. Title
823.9'14 [F]

ISBN 0–7089–4211–3

Published by
F. A. Thorpe (Publishing) Ltd.
Anstey, Leicestershire

Set by Words & Graphics Ltd.
Anstey, Leicestershire
Printed and bound in Great Britain by
T. J. International Ltd., Padstow, Cornwall

This book is printed on acid-free paper

1

He touched her bare shoulder with his finger-tip and then let it move softly up her throat until it reached her lips.

'You're so beautiful.'

Her face relaxed into a smile and he smiled back at her, pleased.

'That's better. You looked despondent!'

She was astonished that he should have read her thoughts so easily.

Sue, Sue, she admonished herself, when will you learn to hide your feelings!

'I'm sorry. It's not true, really. I'm happy!'

She wondered if he knew that was untrue; a white lie because he had been so unselfish in his love-making, so anxious to please her, and the last thing she wanted was to hurt him. There was quite enough hurt floating around the world without . . .

'Don't go away from me. Say something. Tell me what you are thinking.'

She put out a hand and held it for a moment against his cheek. He covered it quickly with his own, holding it there. Gently, she withdrew it, softening the movement with a smile.

'Oh, that you're very good-looking, very attractive, that you are a very macho man.'

He stood up then and pulled on a dressing-gown as if for the first time aware of his nakedness. Then he sat down on the edge of the bed.

She laced her hands behind her head and looked at him. The dressing-gown he wore was too expensive. The column of his throat was firm and strong. Everything about Ross Bryant suggested strength. He could, Sue thought lazily, be the perfect model for a Roman — a gladiator — with rippling muscles and sun-warmed skin turning him into a bronzed statue. His hair was thick and black. It continued to wave — even to curl when wet. He had very dark fine eyes, wide shoulders, narrow hips. A truly handsome man, there was nothing about his physical appearance to suggest he was not as sophisticated as he appeared. He looked as confident and self-possessed as Joe or Paul. She could understand why women fell for him.

She could also see her own reflection in the big gilt framed mirror on the wall opposite the bed. She was by nature modest, never entirely pleased with herself. Paul used to say she had an inferiority complex because she never accepted a compliment from him

2

without shy protest. Strangely, she did not feel shy with Ross. He made her feel more rather than less certain of herself. The mirror reflected her long slim figure with the small waist that Ross could span with his outstretched fingers. Her breasts looked ivory white against the sun tan of her neck and shoulders. But Paul had admired her tapering legs which he thought the most attractive part of her. The mirror was too far away for her to scrutinise her face. There was a tinge of colour in her cheeks; shadows beneath her grey-green eyes that were still outlined with the silver green kohl she had used last night. Her fair thick hair curled untidily about her neck.

Sue looked back at Ross again. He was watching her. He did not seem very happy. He alluded suddenly to her last remark.

'Did you come to bed with me only because I'm physically attractive to you?' His voice had a bitter edge. She was not tactful when she answered:

'Well, yes, in a way.'

Sue closed her eyes as the tears pricked and stung the lids. In the end everything came round full circle to Paul. Even letting herself go to bed with Ross Bryant was because of Paul. Her whole life during the last seven years had been because of Paul.

She conquered her tears. A month of practice was paying dividends. Now, with an effort, she could prevent herself crying. To do so, she had only to force herself to think of something else. She thought now of Ross Bryant. He'd picked her up three nights ago. She and Mary and Joe were staying in the same hotel — the Carleton in La Napoule. He'd waited till her sister, Mary, and Joe, her brother-in-law were on the dance floor and Sue was alone.

'Will you dance this with me?' he had asked.

She would have refused but the band was playing one of Paul's favourite numbers and she was fighting back her tears; so she had nodded and accepted Ross's invitation.

They had exchanged names. She told him she had come here with her sister and brother-in-law for a holiday because she had been ill. They had chosen the Carleton Hotel because Mary and Joe were celebrating the eighth anniversary of their wedding and they had spent their honeymoon here. It had been kind of them to let her be the 'third' because she so badly needed the change.

When Ross asked if she knew this place she told him she had been to Cannes once, but never to La Napoule which was en route for St. Raphael on the Cote d'Azur. Ross agreed

4

La Napoule had great charm. She told him they had all been over the beautiful and famous castle on the water's edge and seen the stone effigies on the tomb in the crypt — effigies of the romantic minded American and his wife who lay there like stone figures in a church, but who had been just an ordinary man and wife who loved each other so dearly they had wished to be buried like this. Charmingly sentimental — so Mary and Joe had thought.

'And you?' Ross had asked curiously, looking down at the beautiful, slightly drawn young face of his dance partner.

Sue had grimaced — wrinkling her nose.

'Romantic nonsense. Things like that don't happen in real life.'

'That is a contradiction — it *did* happen — the two Americans made it happen,' Ross argued. Her cynicism astonished him. She looked so gentle, so feminine. But then women were always surprising Ross.

They had little else to say. They danced gravely, their steps marvellously matched. They neither seemed to want to talk. As the music stopped he left her at her table.

'Who on earth were you dancing with?' Mary asked. Sue had shaken her head and said she didn't know. Joe was interested. He knew the man had a BMW but hadn't any girl with him; Joe had heard him talking in the bar and thought he was an Australian. When Ross came over later to ask for another dance, Mary invited him to join them for a drink. The man looked at Sue, then very politely declined. He was just leaving, thank you, he said, and had thought a final dance would be nice. Sue had danced with him with an indifference Mary did not understand.

Watching her sister, Mary was glad she had made her wear her new dress — a black pleated chiffon with jet straps and jet on the bodice. The long jet earrings she'd lent Sue looked particularly good against her cheeks — particularly good with her fair shining hair brushed up into a high swirl. She wanted Sue to have fun — to laugh and be happy. But Sue, returning to the table once more, seemed as indifferent to her partner as to her own appearance. Ross Bryant left and soon after Sue, too, excused herself and went up to bed.

Preparing for the night, Sue had wondered how Ross Bryant had known she didn't want him at their table; now she knew him better she realised that he was extraordinarily quick to analyse her expressions — to read her thoughts. Such perception struck her as being unusual. It had aroused in her a glimmer of interest in him. The following day, he'd been waiting for her in the lounge of the hotel; had asked her to go out to lunch with him at a different restaurant.

During an excellent meal, Sue learned that his accent was not, after all, Australian as Joe had imagined. It was the first time she'd become conscious of the fact that he came from a different background to her own. She found herself watching closely, judging him. Table manners faultless; a slip when he ordered a sparkling red wine with the pheasant; a few grammatical errors such as when he said 'You and *me*' instead of 'You and *I*'. She became curious about him, forgetting Paul for a few merciful hours; forgetting her own problems as she listened to this new, rather intriguing acquaintance. She took note of many little things about him: the well-chosen Russian leather pocket book with gold corners, the way he flicked out a twenty-pound note casually like a man used to money. There was a cleanliness about him that pleased her; nothing vulgar or over-stated. But he looked a shade nervous when their eyes met. He smiled quickly and it was a warm generous smile, a friendly sort of grin — like a boy's. He told her about himself with a delightful candour.

'My grandfather was the village blacksmith. My dad managed to get me to a grammar school. He was ambitious. He persuaded my grandfather to expand and open a wrought iron side-line to the smithy. It didn't do terribly well — neither my father nor my grandfather having the gift of salesmanship. They made beautiful things but they couldn't sell them, or at least, not far enough afield to make real money.'

'But you saw the possibilities and went on from there?'

'Not at first. I was perfectly happy to leave school at sixteen and go into the business as it was. Then I met a girl. Very beautiful, very aristocratic. Ever so county, I suppose you'd call her. She sometimes used to bring her hunter in to be shod. Of course, there was a groom who could have brought him but she found our place a novelty. I fell madly in love with her; hopelessly, you might well think. It certainly never occurred to me at first that she'd even give me a second look — a brash kid of seventeen. When I realised she was bringing her horse in so she could see me, I was lost. I was so crazy about her I couldn't sleep or eat. One afternoon she left the horse with us and asked me to bring it back to the house when it was re-shod. The look she gave me was a clear invitation. I found her alone, waiting for me in the stable when I got there. I suppose this will sound very naïve but I was

8

only seventeen and sex, such as I knew it, was pretty straightforward. There were girls who 'did' and girls who 'didn't.' The ones who 'did', let you know what they wanted. This girl . . . she made it clear enough. Then, when it was over, she sneered at me; called me a bastard; told me she'd tell her father I'd assaulted her if I ever came near the place again. It threw me. I really was in love with her. I was staggered. Yet I still wanted her like hell. It was a long time before I got around to hating her. That's when I made up my mind — one day I'd get rich enough to put a girl like that in her place and that would be beneath *me*, you understand? I'd never be able to forget the shame of her treatment of me — the cruelty, the humiliation — until I could feel superior to what she was. I started night school, studied economics, advertising, business efficiency. We turned from wrought iron to heavier industry. Steel. Ten years later I was exporting our goods all over the world. I had more money than that girl would ever have.'

Sue was intrigued.

'You saw her again?'

Ross laughed.

'No, by then I didn't give a damn about her. I knew what had happened to her, though. She married into steel; someone who wasn't doing too well at one time. I could have bought him up if I'd wanted. Don't ask me why I didn't. I suppose I just wasn't interested in revenge by then.'

'And you never married?'

'No! That first little affair soured me, ruined more than my pride. She spoilt other women for me — the sort of local girls I might have fallen for and been perfectly happy with. I wanted an aristocratic girl like that first one — her class, if you like. Is that surprising.'

'No, most interesting. I would have thought you'd feel the opposite — hate all of us . . .' Unknowingly Sue put herself on a different level from Ross. 'I suppose subconsciously you still want to possess someone like that girl so that you can feel you've taken a sort of revenge.'

Again, to Sue's surprise, he'd laughed. She began to appreciate his sense of humour. And when he laughed he showed white even teeth. He had a freshness, a clean masculine strength which was attractive.

'No, I have no feelings of revenge. I'm even grateful to her. She opened my eyes to what I was; made me see what potential I had and what could be. Everything I am today I really owe to her.'

That had been during Sue's first lunch with

Ross. Now his voice dragged her back to the present.

'Sue, please don't go away from me. I keep losing you. You're lost to me again in those thoughts of yours.'

She opened her eyes and found him bending over her. She was suddenly faintly aware of the smell of the after-shave lotion he used. His eyes — dark hazel or brown? — were wide and intent. They were bright and sparkling. He had a beautiful body, too. It was easy to understand why the girl on the horse had desired him in her egotistical way. He was so handsome. But he was a stranger. Someone she didn't know yet; certainly didn't love. How could she be here, in bed with him, a man she had not known existed three days ago?

'Sue, whatever it is that is tormenting you, at least tell me you're not sorry we made love.'

'No, of course not. Of course not!'

And in a way, that was true. She wasn't sorry. He'd wanted her so much and it was so easy to say 'yes'; to lie with him and let him love her as he wanted. Something inside her had wanted to prove to him that all girls weren't the same; weren't all hard and cruel enough to call a young boy in love a 'bastard'. It seemed horrible to Sue that such a girl should have been his 'first'.

But somehow what was to have been a one-night-stand had got out of hand. He wouldn't just take what he wanted; he'd wanted her to share all his joy; his complete fulfilment. He had not seemed to realise that she could give him nothing more than a passing physical passion, laced with tenderness because he was nice. Everything she really had to give had been given to Paul. There was nothing, nothing, *nothing* left in her to give to any other man now. She wondered if Ross had guessed just now she was pretending a satisfaction as complete and perfect as his own. Then, quite suddenly, she was too tired to care. She felt Ross's lips on her mouth; lips that were Paul's; Paul's kisses — Paul, *Paul* . . .

She didn't know she was crying, but felt Ross's arms holding her, rocking her like a child. The spectre of loneliness drew back a little. This was why she was in bed with a strange man; for the comfort of his loving; of his need for her, of his uttermost desire. He was yet another way to forget Paul for a few blessed moments of respite; to forget; to forget . . .

Ross went on rocking her in his arms until she slept.

'Joe, wake up. Wake up, Joe!' Mary Deville shook her husband's arm impatiently.

Asleep for only a few minutes, Joe came out of the depths reluctantly. He was a good-looking but too plump man of about forty, with reddish hair, nice blue eyes and a rather loose mouth which spoilt his looks. As he opened one eye, his wife jolted him in the shoulder.

'*Will* you wake up, Joe. This is important. It's Sue!'

Joe groaned. He was bored with Mary's talk about her sister's affairs. For the past month, two weeks at home and two weeks out here in the South of France, he'd heard nothing but talk about Paul Manton and poor Sue's mental state. True, he'd been worried about her himself. Poor little thing had lost a lot of weight and looked utterly miserable; Paul had treated her pretty badly; still, she had to get over it some time and as he said to Mary, the less they all spoke about the past, the better. Forget him and have a good time, he'd said to Sue. There's plenty of other fish in the sea and you're a pretty girl. He thought that these last few days she seemed brighter, perkier, since she'd had Ross Bryant in tow . . .

13

'Now what's the fuss about?' he asked sleepily.

'She's gone, Joe. She isn't in her room. I went along to see if she had any Disprin and she wasn't there.'

'Oh, God, is that all!' he yawned and closed his eyes. 'Probably gone for a walk or something.'

'Joe, will you listen to me?' His wife's pretty face under a layer of moisturizer, was creased with impatience. 'I think she's gone to *his* room. I'm sure of it.'

'*His?*' Joe asked stupidly

'Ross Bryant's, you idiot. I think she's sleeping with him, Joe.'

'So what?' Joe yawned again. 'Jolly good luck to her. Do her the world of good.'

Mary's patience came to an end. She pushed Joe in the shoulder, startling him awake again.

'You're sometimes revolting!' she said furiously. 'And you simply aren't listening to what I'm saying. She's with Ross Bryant, not just a man but with *Ross*!'

'Well, why not with Ross?'

'Are you purposely trying to make me angry? You know what I told you Sue said about him. His grandfather was a blacksmith!'

Joe burst out laughing.

14

'Shouldn't think that's any cause to doubt his ability as a lover!'

Mary stood up, her thin dressing gown gripped tightly in both hands. She stamped her foot.

'You can be as crude as . . . as . . . oh, sometimes I wonder why I married you!' she flared.

Joe held out his arms.

'You're always at your most attractive when you're angry even with that muck on your face. Wipe it off and come to bed, darling. I'll prove I . . . '

'Joe!' Her blue eyes sparkled dangerously. Joe sat up and sighed. Mary, usually so quiet and acquiescent, once on the war-path could go on at him endlessly. If he wanted any sleep . . .

'Look, sweetheart, I honestly don't see what's upsetting you. Sue's twenty-four, old enough to know her own mind, run her own life. Just because you are a few years older and her sister, you can't expect to curtail her sex life as if she was your teenage daughter.'

Mary sank back on the bed and began to wipe her face with a tissue.

'I know that as well as you do, but someone has to look after her. Look at the mess she's made running her own life. Seven long years with a married man. Do you realise she was

15

Paul's mistress longer than I've been your wife?'

'So what does that prove?' Joe asked. 'Only that you were lucky enough to find a chap who wasn't already hooked and Sue wasn't.'

'Oh, I know. I'm not criticising her. When she met Paul she was only seventeen, fresh out of boarding school and about as unworldly as a new born baby. I'll never forgive that man Paul. He's ten years older than Sue. She hadn't a chance. And all the time he kept promising that he would get a divorce, marry her, only not this week, darling; not this month, darling; not this year, darling! God, how I hate that man.'

'On that we are in complete agreement, my love. So what are we arguing about?'

'Only that she can't rush off to bed with any Tom, Dick or Harry. At least Paul was educated. I've forgotten which of the public schools Paul went to, not that it matters really except he did go to one, and to Oxford. He may be an absolute bastard, but at least he came from a good family.'

Joe was grinning again.

'Never thought I'd live to hear you saying something good about Paul Manton!'

'I'll get really angry in a minute,' Mary said, but she turned and looked at Joe anxiously.

16

'I don't want Sue hurt again, Joe. She's had enough to cope with. She really loved Paul. She still loves him. She might weaken and go back to him and I've got to stop that happening.'

Joe sighed.

'Then I suggest you leave the present situation as it is. Seems to me this Ross has come on the scene at the right moment. I don't see why you should think he's going to hurt her. If you ask me, I think he's rather keen on her. Picked her up that first night and has been with her ever since. Lunch yesterday, out all afternoon together, drinks in the evening, swimming this morning, dinner and dancing again tonight.'

'But, Joe, he avoids *us*!'

'Perhaps he doesn't like the look of us!' Joe grinned but remembering Mary was in earnest, added: 'Maybe he's clever enough to realise that you don't approve of his background. Not much point walking into a snub, is there? And *you* are a *snob*, you know you are.'

'I don't think I am in a nasty way,' Mary defended herself. 'I'm not prejudiced. I just don't like the idea of Sue sleeping with a man like that. You can't be too careful these days about who you sleep with.'

'Well, he hardly looks like a drug addict

17

and he's obviously not gay. I'm sure Sue is sensible enough to be taking adequate precautions.'

'I wonder how you'd feel if it was your sister!' Mary said.

'Well, as I haven't a sister, I can't answer that. I just think this is none of your business and that we should both keep our noses out of Sue's personal affairs.'

'But she's so vulnerable at the moment. And she's always been gullible. She's so innocent.' Mary cried.

'Rubbish. No girl can spend seven years as a man's mistress and be innocent,' Joe said caustically. 'Gullible she may be but surely she learned something from her bitter experience. I expect she's just intending to enjoy a little holiday affair to cheer her up.' He yawned, wishing Mary would shut up.

'But Sue isn't like that. She isn't casual or promiscuous. She really *loved* Paul. Right from the start Paul was getting a divorce — his marriage was only hanging together by threads for the sake of the child. Sue wouldn't have let him rent that flat for her, all but move in with her, unless she'd believed him. And there was always some excuse why the divorce was held up; why he had to go home weekends to try and sort things out; lawyer troubles, money troubles, the child was ill — always something, and for years Sue believed every excuse. Then when she finally realized that it was unlikely there would ever be a divorce, she couldn't make the break. She'd given up all her friends — there was nothing but her work and Paul. It takes courage to start again, Joe. Besides, I believe that right up to the end she kept hoping Paul would go through with the divorce and marry her.'

'So! Paul was weak, and untrustworthy, and Sue ended up getting hurt. But it's over now and she's trying to find her feet again. If this man can help her, let him.'

'A man, yes, but not *this* one!' Mary cried, almost in tears. 'There can't be anything permanent about it. She couldn't ever *marry* someone like that.'

'She could. He isn't married. He's got money. That's something these days. Anyway, who says she wants to get married?'

'I know she does, even if she doesn't believe it right now. She's that kind of a girl, Joe. Even when she was quite little she was domesticated, maternal. She's twenty-four now and the best thing in the world would be for her to get married, have a family.'

'Maybe she soon will. There's nothing you can do to hasten it, Mary, so take my advice and keep out of it.'

19

'But Joe, if she gets emotionally involved again, especially to a man like that, no one else is going to come around proposing, are they? And this affair at best can only go on during the time we're out here. When we go home, she'll have to drop him.'

'Because of his accent?' Joe pursed his lips. He didn't approve of this class-conscious twaddle from his wife.

'You're making me sound so beastly, but I suppose his accent is one of the reasons. What on earth do you think Daddy would say; and Mummy, and all our friends, Joe? He just isn't one of us and you know it. He'd be a complete misfit, a social outsider if you like, and I'm not having him drag Sue down to his level.'

'Maybe she could pull him up to ours?' said Joe with another yawn.

'Joe, you know as well as I do that these things still *matter*. I know class is supposed to be dying out in theory but in practice a man like Ross Bryant would be excluded from our circles and you know it. I'll admit having money helps but it won't clear the last ditch.'

'Maybe he doesn't want to clear the last ditch. Maybe Sue wouldn't care, either, if she liked him enough. Personally, I think you're worrying about something which probably will never happen. She's only just met the man to start with so there can't be anything much between them yet; moreover, you told me she's still crazy about Paul Manton. So stop worrying, get into bed and for pity's sake let's get some sleep.'

Mary walked over to the dressing table and lifted a tissue from the box. Thoughtfully she wiped the surplus cream off her face and climbed into bed beside her husband. Joe was already asleep. She switched out the light and lay open-eyed, staring into the darkness.

It's all very well for Joe to talk like that, she thought. He's a man. He didn't see how attractive Ross Bryant was. His face had strength, determination — something more than just good looks. Even she, Mary, had not been blind to the immense sex appeal of such a man. He looked the proverbial Greek God beside some of the thin, short, pallid young men who crowded the Riviera beaches. If only he'd been an Australian maybe he could have got away with his accent. But as things were, Sue just *couldn't* be allowed to fall in love with him.

Grandson of a blacksmith! Mary thought despairingly as at long last she, too, fell asleep.

2

They lay side by side on the rocks, he in the briefest of swimming trunks, she in a white bikini. Neither referred to the previous night until Ross, leaning on one elbow, looked down at her and said suddenly:

'Tell me about Paul.'

She opened her eyes quickly and looked away in the next second, the colour in her cheeks deepening to a blush.

Ross watched her with surprise. Somehow since the moment he had first noticed her in the crowded restaurant of the Carleton, she had been a continual puzzle to him. The most noticeable thing about her as she sat silent and thoughtful at the table with her sister and brother-in-law, had been her air of sadness. She so often looked as though she were re-enacting some private tragedy.

Dancing with her, he'd been surprised to discover that at closer quarters she was even more beautiful than at a distance — far younger and still as sad. He'd half expected her to refuse to dance with him and at first she had hesitated. But the second time he went across to her table, she had got to her

22

feet at once, almost obediently as if she were used to doing what she was told without question. That was when her sister had invited him to join them and he'd seen the unwillingness on Sue's face and declined. He was used to snubs from women of her type; was prepared without surprise or bitterness to accept the fact that this one did not want to further the acquaintance with a man like himself. But as they moved on to the dance floor, Sue had said:

'Thank you — for not accepting my sister's invitation. I'm very tired. After this dance I shall go to bed.'

So it had begun. He remembered the exact moment when he'd realised she was going to become important to him. He'd slept badly, thinking about her constantly and knowing it wasn't just sex. She was attractive, of course, slim, elegant, small-boned with large soft eyes and a creamy flawless skin. Her mouth was full and sensuous, but the face was not sensual. There was an aloofness about it — a delicate fastidiousness. If there was passion, it was hidden beneath a façade of cool reserve, which was not, however, unfriendly. There was a gentle quality — a moving shyness about her sudden smile.

In the morning he had found himself far more anxious than he would have believed possible that she should agree to lunch with him. Yet when she had nodded an unsmiling agreement, he had been surprised at her readiness to do so. He wasn't a particularly vain man but he knew that he was attractive to women — to most of them, anyhow. But he had no illusions about the female sex nor indeed about himself. This girl, he could judge with intuition, was interested in him, yet it was not because of this that she had accepted his company. Why it was he did not really know; any more than he knew why she had let him kiss her; and why, most of all, she had allowed him to take her to bed.

He bent closer to her now.

'Don't you want to talk about *him* — Paul, I mean?'

He saw her throat move as she swallowed. She was nervous. But she gave the smallest shrug of the shoulders and answered:

'I suppose I did the unforgivable and called you by Paul's name?'

He nodded, unsmiling.

'Well, I'm sorry!' She did not sound as if she really were sorry. She sounded almost deliberately flippant and casual. Yet he was sure she was far from being one of the promiscuous 'sleep-with-any-man-who-wants-me' kind.

24

He waited. Soon she said in a hard, cool voice:

'Paul is the man I've been living with for the last seven years. I suppose it was inevitable I should make that mistake.' Suddenly she paused and looked at Ross, her face softening. She went on more gently. 'I'm really sorry. And I never thanked you for putting me back in my bed!'

Again he was shocked. In the course of his life, he'd met all kinds of people from all walks of life. He was no prude. For some men the easy way they treated sex and women was all right. It couldn't be like that for him. He had to have more than a pretty body and an empty mind before he could feel utterly satisfied and at peace. What the girl was, was far more important to him than how she looked. This one — he just couldn't see her not caring what the man was like, either; despite last night. Fantastic though it seemed, he could only think of Sue as innocent — strangely, touchingly so.

'Seven years is a long time,' he said thoughtfully. 'Is it . . . over now?'

Her voice trembled as she replied:

'Yes, it's over! I loved him very much. He was my whole life.'

Ross felt a sudden flash of jealousy — a new emotion for him.

'And he loved you, of course?'

Her laugh was bitter.

'Oh, there's no 'of course' about it. He did at first . . . I really think he did love me at first.' She looked at Ross without really seeing him and talked now as to herself. 'I was a silly inexperienced schoolgirl when I first met Paul. He helped me grow up, become a woman. He did love me then. Yes, I really believe he did.'

'He was older than you, I suppose. Didn't he want to marry you?'

She laughed painfully.

'Oh, he was married already. The marriage was supposed to be on the rocks when we first met. He was getting a divorce. I think, in fact, he was going through a sticky patch. Melanie, his wife, was having an affair with someone else. Paul had evidence. But he never acted on it. There was always a delay, lawyer trouble, money trouble, Melanie ill, the child ill — difficult . . . It went on for years. Then Melanie found out about me . . . at least, I've always imagined she did. Suddenly she wanted Paul back. Of course he'd never really left her in the physical sense. He used to live at the flat during the week and went home at weekends. I wonder if you know how lonely London can be on a Saturday and Sunday?'

26

It was a rhetorical question and he did not answer. He felt her pain, her bitterness yet he knew this was not the time for sympathy. For the moment, she needed just to talk.

'What was he like?' he asked, his curiosity combined with a preconceived dislike for the man.

'Paul? Oh, good-looking in a thin aristocratic way; you know what I mean — the sort of lean hungry look and a long thin nose. He had a very beautiful mouth — like a girl's. Mary said it was a weak mouth. I suppose it was really. But it was beautiful. His hands, too — long, thin, tapering. He's in the Foreign Office as matter of fact. I suppose even these days a messy divorce wouldn't be popular there.'

He admired her attempt to be flippant again; her gallant attempt to show she didn't really care after all.

'He's doing very well, I believe. I can imagine it, too. You always had to believe Paul, whatever he was saying. He always made everything sound so plausible. Or perhaps I was just easily fooled. Mary says I am a fool. Poor Mary. She does worry about me.'

'I'm afraid she doesn't like me very much!'

Now Sue smiled.

'What nonsense, Ross. She'd like you very

much if she knew you.'

'Somehow I doubt it. This morning when I went in to breakfast, she cut me dead. Your brother-in-law smiled, but your sister gave him a fearful dig in the ribs, poor man. I'll bet anything you like she was muttering: 'Don't encourage him!"

'Ross, you are an idiot!'

He let her continue to think he was joking. He did not want anything to wipe that smile from her face. But in fact he knew Sue's sister was going to mean trouble with a capital T.

'Ross . . . ' her voice was hesitant, sounding embarrassed. 'I . . . I'm not sorry . . . about last night, I mean, but I . . . well, I wanted you to know . . . I won't again.'

'I see!' Now it was his turn to hide his bitterness. So he had just been a quick fling, a one-night-stand.

'Ross, I want you to understand. It isn't because of you — it's Paul. I'm still in love with him, you see. So I've nothing genuine to give. That's why I can't pretend. I have to be able to respect myself — or rather my motives for certain actions in my life. Can you see what I'm driving at?'

He could and he felt an enormous sense of relief. He put out a hand and clasped Sue's tightly in his own.

'You're not to worry about anything at all,'

he said. 'There's nothing you have to do — or nothing you can't do. Only one important thing matters — that you should be happy.'

He lay back on the rock, his face turned to the sun. 'We'll swim again in a minute, if you like.'

Sue sat watching him. In so far as it was possible for her to think about anyone at all but Paul, she was curious about Ross. He was the first self-made man she had come in contact with personally. Her childhood with Mary in a large country house in Kent had followed the usual middle-class pattern with 'suitable' friends found by their parents for them to play with; 'suitable' boarding schools at which they met girls from the same sort of background. Local dances were never even contemplated. Such parties as there were, were given by friends of their parents. In a way, it had been a sheltered childhood; too sheltered. When she'd left her boarding school, aged seventeen, she'd known little about men. Paul had come into her life like a fairy-tale prince. For one wonderful week, everything had been like a romantic novel; Paul 'phoning; Paul coming to dinner; Mummy and Daddy liking and approving of the young diplomat; encouraging them both.

Then it happened — Mother discovering Paul was married. Sue was forbidden to see him again. Paul was forbidden to write or 'phone. Remembering those days Sue could see how her parents had added fuel to the fire within her. The fact that she and Paul were forbidden to meet made their secret assignations the more romantic, desperate, desirable. Paul had been clever. He was the one who'd thought up the secretarial course in London so that she had to share a flat there with a cousin who didn't ask questions. Paul had found a flat for himself: told his wife he was too busy to get back to Berkshire during the week. At first, Sue had only visited the flat; spent long evenings lying in Paul's embrace, saying 'No!' with decreasing fervour. Paul gave her no peace. He told her again and again that if she really loved him, she would let him make love to her. He needed her so desperately. His marriage was on the rocks; his wife had been unfaithful. He had no loyalties toward her. It was only a matter of time before he would be free to marry Sue. Meanwhile, they had to keep the affair secret from her parents. Sue's family would never approve of him until he was divorced from Melanie. If only she were not so young, Paul kept arguing, she would understand how he felt about her. So young . . . *too young* . . .

Then she wasn't young any longer. The

schoolgirl's romantic dreams were gone and replaced by a passion more than equal to Paul's. Within six months she had finished her secretarial course. Sue told her parents she had found a job in London. Paul had a friend who ran a travel agency who gave her a reasonably paid job. He wrote her a letter to show her parents, confirming the fact that he was employing her. She moved in 'with another girl' in order to be nearer her work. Paul himself wrote as 'the other girl', signing himself 'Daphne'. The few times her mother called at the flat 'Daphne' was away. All very convenient and feasible.

Sue had been afraid at first. Then the long moments of doubt passed. It was easy — too easy. Her parents accepted all the lies without question. Sue went home every weekend while Paul, down in his own home, tried to see what could be done to expedite proceedings for his divorce. Sue hated the weekends. The partings on Saturday mornings became unbearable. She began to feel she could not leave the flat at weekends because every nook and corner of it was as much a part of Paul as of herself. Then Mummy began to worry and Mary was sent to investigate. Mary arrived without warning one Sunday when, after a bit of clever scheming on Paul's part, he'd managed to stay with Sue over the Saturday. They were in bed.

Remembering, Sue's cheeks burned. For the first time she had felt more than guilt. She was embarrassed and shamed that her sister should have discovered her *in flagrante delicto* and found out her tissue of lies. Mary had been decent. She'd said she wouldn't tell their parents if Sue gave Paul up.

'It isn't because you are living with him, Sue. You're nearly nineteen now and I reckon a girl has to make her own life at your age. It's because Paul's married. There's no future in it. He's no good to you, Sue darling. He's just taking all you've got to give and giving nothing real or lasting in return.'

Poor Mary! She had tried so hard. She never did tell but they found out anyway because the porter in the block of flats where Sue lived let the truth out. That had been the day her mother called to see Sue and she was out.

'Mrs Manton should be back by lunch time!' he'd said, trying to be helpful. He'd let Sue's mother into the flat. She had found all Paul's clothes — his drinks and cigars — and so much other evidence that her 'little Sue' was living with a man and that 'Daphne' was a myth. When Sue returned home, her mother said:

'Give him up or your Father and I will have nothing more to do with you!'

Sue chose to stay with Paul. He was everything now. She lived for the hours he spent with her, utterly dependent upon him emotionally. *Too* dependent.

Paul became restless. He began to go home more often — Friday nights instead of Saturday mornings; returning Monday mornings instead of Sunday nights. There would be occasional days in the week when he found excuses to go home — his child's birthday; his wife's dinner party. And a few others.

They argued hotly about the divorce. Again and again Paul explained that he couldn't rush things. First he had to get evidence against Melanie; he must be the one to bring the action. If Sue loved him she must understand that. There was the money side of it, too; he couldn't keep two homes going if Melanie claimed alimony. Leave it to him, he begged Sue. Be patient. It would all work out. When he made love to her later, she believed all that he said. But later still, she was sick with doubt again. Did Paul really love her? Did he really mean to get a divorce at all? How much longer could she tolerate this lack of security?

Well, she had gone on another four years,

four years that became increasingly unhappy and unsatisfactory for her. There were times when she did in fact pack up and leave the flat and Paul. She went to Mary's with her luggage, really meaning to end the agony which had swamped all joy.

Then Paul wrote, telephoned, pleaded and she was lost again. Nothing mattered if he really loved and needed her. Even marriage didn't matter. Even sharing him with Melanie didn't matter — so long as she could stay in his life and in his arms.

God, what a fool! she thought today as all the bitter memories crowded back and suffocated her. She felt unable to bear her bitterness but her thoughts were interrupted as Ross pulled her to her feet saying 'I'll race you to the beach'.

She dived quickly into the limpid clear sea and swam after him. He was a strong swimmer and was waiting on the shore, her towel held out, his dark eyes sparkling in the sunshine — his brown body diamond bright with water.

'Why, thank you!' she said, surprised at his thoughtfulness. Paul had never been a man to make such charming gestures — it was always she, Sue, who had spoiled him — thought about him.

Ross's face suddenly darkened.

'We don't necessarily have bad manners!' he snapped.

'We?' She did not understand his meaning.

'People of my class!' Ross said, his voice unusually rough. She was quick to sense his sensitivity — to understand how careful one had to be not to hurt this man's feelings.

'Oh, Ross!' She sat down on the sand beside him and let her hand rest gently on his arm. She felt the muscles stiffen at her touch but let her hand remain. 'It's just that I'm not used to being looked after. I've noticed several times you open doors for me; you fetch a cushion for me. You worry if I don't have exactly what I like to eat. I'm afraid you are spoiling me and . . . well, I just wanted you to know that I do notice these things and . . . well, that I'm grateful. It's all very new and delightful for me, I assure you.'

She saw that his brow cleared and his smile returned. He turned and covered her hand with his. She noticed how large it was, brown, muscular, the fingers square and blunt; hands so different from Paul's. He was altogether different. Maybe that was why it was possible for her to be with him. In every way, he was Paul's opposite. She looked at his strong, rugged, handsome face. He looked directly back into her eyes as though he were about to reply. But he only said:

'The water is nice. Perfect temperature.'

She wondered what he really wanted to say. Then her thoughts wandered again. Since her final parting with Paul, she'd found it terribly difficult to concentrate on anything for long. Her sister — ever kind and anxious — insisted she was having a nervous breakdown. Her doctor advised complete rest. She didn't really care about her life much one way or the other. It was Mary's idea she should go away with Joe and herself for a holiday. The South of France would be a complete change, just what Sue needed for recuperation. As if anywhere in the world there existed a medicine to cure a broken heart!

'If you'd just get around to hating Paul,' Mary had said as they flew to Nice, 'you might start being happy again. God knows you've enough reason to hate him. Seven bloody wasted years!'

'But they weren't wasted, Mary.'

'Oh, yes, they were. None of that twaddle about love is never wasted! Of course they were. What have you got to show for it all? Not a friend, not a job, not a husband, a family. One broken heart — that's all Paul Manton gave you. I can't understand why you don't loathe his guts.'

If I could, Sue thought, there might be an

36

end to pain and I could stop crying every time I hear a tune he liked. I might stop thinking all the time about him. Paul will be leaving the office now, half past five. He'll be on the Underground; he'll be turning the corner of the street: he'll be saying 'Good evening' to old Banks by the lift. He'll be in the lift, his key will be in the door and I'll hear it scrape and turn and my heart will turn over like the key and — '

'Sue!'

She was crying again, not noisily but silently, the tears dripping slowly down her cheeks, mingling with the sea water.

She lay down on the warm sand, burying her face in her towel, ashamed of her lack of control. That was always her trouble, no self-control. How many times had Paul said: 'Now for pity's sake, Sue, don't start crying . . . ' 'For the love of God, don't look so bloody pathetic, so accusing, so help-less . . . '.

'Sue, I want to tell you about myself. Will you listen? I want your advice about something.'

Ross's quiet, yet strong, clear voice with its unfamiliar accent, penetrated her thoughts again. She struggled against the tears and nodded.

'I've no background, an uneducated voice,

as you know, no old school tie, no entrée to the best clubs, no friends among the 'best' people. I can buy my way into a few so-called 'right' circles. Not that I mind . . . I've grown up pretty used to social snobbery, I assure you. But now I feel differently. I do mind, not for myself, but because I'm in love with a girl from those 'right' circles. I want to know what *you* think I should do about it? Give her up, knowing nothing can come of it? Hope that one day she might love me enough not to mind my disadvantages? Face the fact that if I want to marry, it'll have to be to a girl from my own background? What do you think, Sue?'

Despite herself she was attentive now. Of all he had said, she was most surprised to hear he was in love with someone. After last night . . . but then, of course, last night had only been a casual affair for her, so why not for him?

'I wonder if you really are in love with this girl,' Sue said, aloud, 'or if you aren't getting confused by your feelings about the past — the old hurts and insults.'

'Oh, no. I'm really in love — for the first time in my life. It's the first time I've ever been in love and it's very obvious to me. Now I realise that what I felt for other women is utterly different from what I feel now. I didn't want it to happen but I could not prevent it — it happened in spite of me.'

'Well, then why the problem? If you love her you can't give her up without an effort to get her. Besides, what makes you think she'll care about the differences in your backgrounds? Maybe she doesn't care. Lots of people don't.'

He twisted his lips and narrowed his eyes.

'Don't they? Maybe among the so-called arty people — the literary circles, musicians and such. Nice big-hearted friendly types. But 'class' matters a hell of a lot to some of your county crowd.'

'Does it? It ought not to. To me what counts is what a person is, not where they come from. Anyway, you're exaggerating things, Ross. You're not all that different. The difference is not as noticeable as you imagine. It's become an obsession with you.'

'You say that because in your frame of mind, you aren't aware of anything much but your own feelings. You obviously haven't gathered that your sister is worried about your friendship with me.'

'Oh, Mary! She's always worrying about me. Forget it, Ross. Tell me about your girl friend — the one you love. Where does she come from.'

'Your sort of background. That's why I

asked you, Sue. And your answer is important to me. If you fell for a man like me — that is if you ever could fall in love with a man like myself, would you care about his upbringing?'

'What a horrible question! How can I answer? I just don't know, Ross. Such a lot would depend on . . . well, how big the differences were between us. I mean, if he was really rough, had terrible manners — if he didn't bath often or something like that — then I don't think I'd ever fall for him in the first place. Take little things like the way one talks to waiters,' Sue laughed. 'The way you hear some men talk too loudly and everyone in the restaurant can hear them! That kind of thing would undoubtedly embarrass me and put me off. It would depend on the kind of friends I had, too. I mean, if they were all intellectual and this man was only able to talk about how much he'd paid for a heifer or something, or make terrible blunders and gaffs, it would all be really embarrassing, for me. But then you don't qualify on any of those counts, Ross.'

'Then you wouldn't be ashamed to go out with me?'

She tossed back her wet hair and grinned at him.

'Idiot — of course not. But marriage is

another question, isn't it? Married couples live at such close quarters. Even a small habit can become magnified when one has to put up with it day in and night out. It's all a question of the amount the two concerned differ, though I suppose it ought not to if one really *is* in love. I'm trying to be honest, Ross, and honestly, I don't know the answer. I might fall in love with some sort of man everyone else would hate. I don't know. You've got to sort out your own problems. I can't really give a fair answer.'

'You're a very honest person,' said Ross slowly, his eyes half-closed, appraising her. 'That's one of the things I like about you.'

'I think honesty is important — one of the most important things in life. Even if the truth hurts sometimes, it's better than a lie. For instance, if Paul hadn't *pretended* he meant to marry me, and if I hadn't pretended to myself that one day he would . . . ' She paused, the colour suddenly draining from her face. She turned away from him.

'You must stop thinking about him. It's not the least bit flattering to me!' Ross's voice was teasing gently. It brought a sudden apologetic curve to Sue's lips. She smiled again.

'You're right. All the same, you weren't being very complimentary either. All this about some girl you've fallen in love with. Oh well, carry on, Big Lover. Is she in love with *you*? Tell me more about her.'

Ross gave her a long, speculative look.

'She's in love with someone else — someone who made her very unhappy; someone who didn't begin to know how to love her, protect her. But despite this he is all she can think about. She's very beautiful and very lonely and — oh, hell — I love her as I never thought I'd love any woman in this world,' he ended. The expression in his eyes was unmistakable.

Now she understood. Embarrassment, confusion and surprise made her speechless. At last she managed to speak and chose to keep up the pretence about the mythical girl.

'I expect you're just sorry for her because she's been such a fool, made a mess of everything. You . . . you're a very chivalrous person and you want to help her. That doesn't mean you love her, Ross. You couldn't love anyone you'd known so short a time . . . and anyway, it would be quite pointless since she's still in love with this other man and always will be. I'm so sorry, Ross.'

He didn't touch her, but his face was so near to her she could see the dark gold flecks in his brown eyes. He didn't look unhappy, she thought, but serious — disturbingly so.

He said:

'Sue, I'm the one who is sorry. I shouldn't have bothered you with my problems. Anyway, they aren't important. But I'm glad you know, even if it doesn't mean anything to you. I know you're still in love with Paul. I know that what happened last night was only your way of trying to escape your memories. I can understand. But for the first time in my life, I find a girl more important to me than myself. It is important to me that everything should be as *you* want it. I suppose I've been pretty selfish in the past whenever I've made love to a woman. I wanted her. I took her if she was willing, and if she found equal pleasure in the moment, then to me, also, it was incidental. But although I want you more than I've ever wanted a woman before, when we were together, if you'd given me even the smallest indication that you didn't want *me*, I'd have backed off. It's the same now. I'm dying to kiss you, hold you, but only if you want me to. So you see, I'm not asking anything more from you than you want to give. If you want to forget the past, then at least let me achieve that for you. I'll try and work the miracle.'

She looked at him with despair in her eyes.

'You're so nice, Ross, but I have to be honest with you. I like you very much and maybe if things had been different I could have fallen in love with you. But I'm no good to any man. I'm empty, Ross — quite empty. I've nothing to give. I'm in a kind of vacuum and I can't seem to care for anyone or about anything. I'd be sorry if our friendship had to end but I wouldn't really *care*. Do you understand? I like being with you but it's only because while I am, you stop me thinking about Paul. That's mean of me and selfish but it's true. My mind tells me how nice you are; how flattered I ought to be that you think you love me; but here . . . ' she touched her heart, ' . . . here I feel nothing at all. So you see, if you think maybe it's worth while you going on seeing me — just in case I change my mind, it's useless. I've left Paul. I don't suppose I'll ever see him again. But the day I left him, I also left behind my capacity for love. I was with him too long, Ross. No other man can replace him. I don't even want another man to replace him. I don't want ever to love anyone again — ever. So I don't want to be made to feel emotional about you. Do you see how hopeless it is? I've nothing to give, nothing.'

To her surprise, Ross did not seem in the least surprised by her outburst. He said gently:

'Well, now we've both put our cards on the table we can start on a firm basis. We know

44

the truth about each other and all the odds.'

'How do you mean 'start on a firm basis'?' Sue questioned. He smiled. 'Start our friendship. I understand that you can't love me but that needn't stop us being friends?'

Surprised — touched — she replied:

'It's true I need a friend. So long as friendship really is all you want, Ross?'

'I want anything I can get from you,' he said and she read the candour, the sincerity in his eyes. 'Friendship is no small gift. In the end, I'm not at all sure it isn't more important than love. Love has a way of wearing out — real friendship lasts a life-time. And you know, I haven't many friends — only associates. My own people resent my having stepped up in the world and my financial success. And in your circle I'm on sufferance. When I'm not too busy to think about it, I realise that I'm a very lonely man.'

'Then we're both lonely!' Sue said. 'Perhaps that's what we really have in common.'

Slowly Ross got to his feet, pulling her up beside him. He stood for a moment, his big hands lightly holding her thin delicate arms.

'Maybe we need each other, Sue!' he said, smiling. 'And that's enough for me. Now come and lunch with me. I want to see you

45

put on some weight.'

He gathered up their belongings and linking his arm through hers, helped her carefully up the rocky path towards the hotel.

Sue's sister stood on the terrace of the Carleton, watching them approach.

It won't do! she told herself grimly. No matter what Joe says, I've got to stop this somehow before it's too late.

3

The day was brilliant.

The end of June was nearly always perfect in the South of France. Sue had allowed herself to be persuaded to drive to Eze. Ross had hired the BMW for the fortnight he was down here. She'd learned quickly that Ross Bryant never did anything by halves. It made her a little uneasy to see so much money recklessly thrown around. On the other hand she did not feel he did so ostentatiously. It seemed rather to spring from a childishly endearing wish to be generous; and from pleasure at having nowadays the means to be so.

She enjoyed the drive through Cannes and Nice and along the winding Corniche road leading to Monte Carlo. Soon after leaving Beaulieu behind them they were at the wrought iron gates of one of the loveliest hotels on the *Cote d'Azur* — the Cap Estel.

'Someone I know who plays golf with me recommended it but I couldn't get in this year — that's what sent me to La Napoule — luckily,' Ross told her when Sue said how glorious she thought Cap Estel.

Ross laid his left hand lightly on her knee. She did not push it away. His touch was friendly rather than sensuous. He looked good in his pale blue sports shirt and the blue fisherman's trousers which he told her he had bought on a holiday in Capri.

There was something tremendously warm and strong about this man; so utterly different from Paul. Unwittingly, she was making comparisons. Paul was more slender and aesthetic. His passion, when he exhibited it, always came as a surprise to her because of the cool façade behind which he hid his emotions. There was something aloof and mysterious about Paul that made Sue try to probe the depths — solve the mystery — get closer to him. With Ross it was very different. His personality was warm and enveloping, extroverted; his feelings showing readily on the surface.

Ross parked his car outside the hotel — a long low white villa rather like a wedding cake, Sue thought, amused. It was once the home of a foreign prince who had built it for an adored bride. When she died he sold it.

Sorrow and disaster were never far away, she reflected as she remembered the couple who lay in the tomb in the castle of La Napoule.

Ross tucked an arm through hers and

walked with her into the hotel, then out onto the broad white, flower-filled terrace. They carried their swimwear with them. They had to descend steep white marble steps to the tables under the trees. Ross ordered coffee. Then he led her down past the swimming pool, along a winding path to the Cap Estel private beach.

Sue looked to him so young in her white shirt and shorts, her fair hair glistening in the sun, that he was sorry she had to change. He didn't want her to leave him even for the few minutes she took to get into her bikini. He felt his heart surge with a great wave of desire when he saw her walking toward him where he sat on the pebbled shore, waiting for her.

God, she was beautiful, he thought. He liked the proud way in which she moved, the way she lifted her heart-shaped face and smiled.

I'm hopelessly in love with her, Ross Bryant said to himself. It gets worse every minute.

They dived off the rocks into the limpid waters, and came up laughing at each other, half blinded and dazzled by the sun. Sue felt she was slipping back to childhood, swimming, ducking under water, ready to catch the hand that Ross held out. He shouted to her: 'Race you out to the raft.' He was there long before her. He was a powerful swimmer and she had not recovered her lost energies.

After their swim they returned to the hotel to lunch under the trees. Sue noticed several women looking at Ross and was amused and pleased.

The meal was ordered by Ross. She found it rather touching that he made sure each course would be what *she* wanted. She was so used to Paul saying: 'I know exactly what we're going to have today.'

They ate fresh scampi, veal, then an orange sorbet. Sue had never tasted it before — an orange water-ice served inside fresh fruit. Ross wanted her to drink champagne but she refused. He pressed her for a reason. Gently she explained that her father, a real gourmet, had told her never to drink champagne with good food. She suggested an iced hock. Ross did not seem in the least put out by her reply. He just nodded thoughtfully and ordered the wine.

Soon they were both laughing at Ross's execrable French. It was heavily punctuated with English but he took care to keep his voice down when he spoke to the waitress. She noted also, his over-generous tipping.

When they had finished their coffee, Ross asked:

'Do you want to get back to La Napoule this afternoon?'

'Definitely not.'

'Shall we swim again?'

She nodded, smiling. She felt less unhappy than she had been for weeks. During one whole morning she had scarcely thought of Paul.

At her request they lay on mattresses on the beach for a while, their heads in the shade of a striped umbrella. Ross, reclining on his stomach, head on one side, could not take his gaze from her. He paid her lavish compliments, covering his seriousness with deliberate extravagance.

'I've never seen such a wonderful mouth on any woman. I want to kiss you, Sue.'

'Don't, you make me self-conscious,' she laughed.

'You're really beautiful,' he said. 'At least, to me you are. I can't take my eyes off you.'

She laughed again. This wasn't serious. It was fun.

'After our swim this morning and that meal, I feel sleepy, but I can't sleep if you talk so much,' she murmured.

He shut his eyes and surprisingly was fast asleep in a matter of seconds. She found that amusing. She was half inclined to dig him in the ribs and accuse him of being bored with her, then smiled softly to herself and refrained.

But he was only cat-napping. Within minutes he opened his eyes and moving nearer to her, took her hand and carried it to his lips. She did not pull her hand away. The clasp of his fingers was strangely comforting.

Deliberately she kept her thoughts away from the future. Soon now, she would be going back to England, to London . . . a London in which Paul, also, would be. Here it was possible to put Paul out of her thoughts but once she was within 'phoning distance . . .

She forced herself to concentrate on the man beside her. She hoped very much that he wasn't really in love with her; that this little interlude in their lives meant just that for him, too. She didn't want him to be hurt; to be inadvertently the one to hurt him. She was unhappily conscious that in a way she had been making use of him. That wasn't fair — because she genuinely liked him.

'He's old enough to take care of himself!' she told herself sharply. He was no young boy but very much a man of the world. She'd been honest with him at the start — told him she wished to stay emotionally uninvolved. It was up to him to keep this holiday flirtation on a light note and not to make more of it than that. When they went back to England, she probably would not see him again. She sighed, a little of the day's happiness ebbing away. Life could so quickly become complicated. Until now her friendship with Ross had allowed her to stay uninvolved. She did not want to feel responsible for him. It was entirely his own fault if, despite her warnings, he had allowed himself to fall in love.

For the remainder of the afternoon she was cool and distant with him, leaving him puzzled and confused by the sudden transition from the morning's friendliness. He drove her back to the hotel in silence, miserably afraid that after a few days in his company, she had finally become bored by him.

He did not ask her to dine with him. Instead, very much alone and a little frightened by the strength of his feelings, he went out by himself and deliberately got very drunk on bad champagne.

★ ★ ★

The sisters were in Sue's bedroom.

'You mean you told him about Paul? You must be out of your mind. One would have thought you'd be ashamed to tell a virtual stranger that you've lived . . . ' Mary broke off with a helpless shrug of her shoulders.

' 'In Sin', no doubt you want to say,' finished Sue on an ironic note.

The packing was done. Tomorrow they were going home . . . back to London. Mary, determined to speak to Sue before they left, had finally managed to corner her for a private talk. Somehow lately Sue had managed to avoid 'heart to hearts' with her sister. Now sitting at her dressing table, brushing her hair with slow, thoughtful strokes, Sue was cornered. Mary had come in unexpectedly. There was no avoiding her accusations.

'He isn't a stranger to me,' Sue said quietly. 'Nor would he be to you if you weren't such a snob. He can't help his background any more than we can help ours. You haven't even tried to get to know him. He's a very charming man.'

Mary sat down on the bed, her eyes full of distress.

'I may be a snob but you're the one who preaches the necessity of facing facts!' she said pointedly. 'And what are the facts? Ross Bryant just isn't our class. He doesn't move in our crowd, nor will he ever do so no matter how much money he makes. Can you see Daddy welcoming him as a son-in-law? Or Mummy dining with him? They'd have a fit if they knew you had taken up with a man like him. And so would our other relations and most of our friends and you know it. There may be the odd exception, people like Joe who is so easy-going he doesn't care much about speech or uncouth manners . . . '

'Ross is not uncouth!' Sue quickly defended him.

'Well, he's not a gentleman,' argued Mary. 'Oh, I grant you Joe wouldn't mind. He likes any chap with whom he can have 'fun'. He thinks it's fun to tell a lot of coarse jokes and muck around with shop girls and waitresses. Oh, I've no illusions about Joe . . . give him half a chance and he'd drop all *his* standards for a few hours' amusement. It's a good thing he has someone like me behind him or goodness knows what levels he'd sink to. It's always been a sore point with me.'

Mary at school had been the neat, clean, obedient little girl who won the goodwill and approval of her teachers and had excellent reports; passed all her exams with the greatest ease. The studious well-behaved girl became a dull young woman, but she had a very good figure and a fine pair of blue eyes, and Joe Deville fell in love with her. They met at the tennis club, went in for tournaments together. Before Joe quite knew what had happened Mary had him at the altar.

With his usual casual good-nature, Joe accepted marriage as inevitable sooner or later and he was genuinely fond of Mary — looked up to her as a great deal more sensible and level-headed than himself. She had proved to be a good wife.

Sue, brushing her hair, considered Mary's marriage. She knew it hadn't been altogether a bed of roses. Despite his education and respectable upbringing, Joe remained the eternal schoolboy. He refused to take life seriously. He could have gone a lot further in his father's business if he'd been prepared to settle down and work. But Joe liked the easy way; he liked to get away from the office as soon as he could, join the men at the bar, nip off for an afternoon's golf, throw away a week's salary at the races. He was always buying a new car, something sporty, fast, that took his fancy.

There had been girls, too. Everyone hoped when Mary married him, Joe would settle down and become a little more responsible. Mary was cool, level-headed and much the stronger character. But she hadn't been able to prevent Joe's occasional indiscretions. Sensibly, she accepted his infidelities for the casual unimportant affairs they were to him. A girl in a strip-tease club; a pretty typist. Joe hadn't really cared about either one. Mary had overlooked them and Joe had sworn each time it wouldn't happen again. Both of them knew that it probably would.

'He'll grow up one of these days!' Mary always said with far more nonchalance than she really felt at the time. Joe's weaknesses were the reason Mary hadn't had children. 'He can't look after himself,' she had once told Sue bitterly, 'let alone take on the responsibilities of a family. And anyway, I have my hands full looking after him!'

'Mary, please don't worry,' Sue suddenly appealed to her sister, anxious not to add to Mary's worries. Mary had been a wonderful sister, despite her apparent hardness. She'd stood by throughout the affair with Paul, which Mary had never understood and never approved. She'd been there when the crash came. Without Mary, Sue didn't know what she would have done. The anguish was still not far away.

'Don't let me be weak and go back to him!' she had cried, Mary's arms holding her tightly. And Mary had answered the 'phone for her, burnt Paul's letters and arranged for Sue to come away on holiday with them. Mary had paid Sue's expenses, too. She and Joe were comfortably off. Joe earned a reasonable salary and had a bit of capital. There was no family to support. All the same, not every sister would have done as much, and Sue knew it. She could forgive and understand it when Mary stopped being patient and tolerant.

Now Mary sighed.

'How can I help worrying about you? I know it's none of my business but I'm not blind or an idiot and I know you've been to bed with that man. I just can't understand how you *could*, Sue. Paul . . . well, he was attractive. I could understand a girl losing her head over him. But Ross Bryant . . . goodness!'

'Isn't he attractive?' Sue could not prevent a smile. 'Other women seem to find him so.'

'Oh, do be sensible for once, Sue. You know very well what I mean. I *grant* he's good looking. But it's what he *is* . . . '

'So that damns him in your eyes. You're a first rate snob, Mary!'

Mary flushed angrily.

'Snob I may be, but the whole thing is quite beyond my comprehension. You can't possibly fall in *love* with a man like Ross Bryant.'

'I don't love him. He knows that. He's just my friend, Mary, and God knows I need a good friend. He's been wonderful company for me this holiday. There have even been times when he's made me forget Paul.'

Mary's face softened.

'I know, darling. But that's one of the reasons I'm worried. You're so vulnerable right now. I should think any man in the world who's the least bit kind to you would be able to catch you on the rebound. That's why I've got to lecture — warn you. You made a hell of a mess of your life by letting Paul run it. Now you've finally left him to make a fresh start and here you are, landing yourself in a worse mess with an even less suitable man. The sort you should get friendly with now are the kind you could marry.'

Sue drew a breath that was largely a tired sigh.

'I don't *want* to get married, Mary, or to fall in love again. Ross offers me friendship with no strings attached. I'm not committed in any way. I may or may not see him once we get back to London. Probably I shall, because I like being with him. As to being 'caught on the rebound', there isn't a man living I'd go to the altar with at the moment. Odd though you may think me — I'm still in love with Paul. It won't be easy when we do get home. If Paul telephones or writes to me, it'll be the same old battle. Every nerve in my body cries out to go back to him. I know I mustn't and I won't, but I still want to. He's the only man I ever want to marry. So maybe I did sleep with

Ross. Do you think it was because I wanted him? It was because I wanted Paul.'

Mary, torn between her dislike of what she heard and her pity for her sister, let the latter win.

'Darling, hush!' She put a hand on the slim, trembling shoulders. 'I know it's hell and I don't want to deny you any comfort that's offered — although it's so *dangerous*! If Ross can help you, I suppose it is better than nothing. But you're going to have to work, Sue, find an interesting job — something to fill in the time, stop you brooding. It shouldn't be difficult with your secretarial training behind you. Thank God at least you have that.'

Sue turned from her sister. She had recovered her control.

'Ross has offered me a job,' she said. 'I told him I'd think about it. It's in his London office where they deal with most of the big contracts. He says they are always short of good secretaries and the ones they get are usually bimbos. If I can cope, there's a good chance of speedy promotion.'

Mary looked at her younger sister dubiously. Sue certainly looked a lot better than she had done when they arrived at La Napoule three weeks ago. Through the brown tan one could see faint colour in her cheeks, although she was normally pale. She'd lost that desperate angular thinness — put on weight and she was less tense, not so much on edge. Maybe this man was good for her, Mary thought sighing. If Sue had no intention of falling in love with him, it didn't much matter what kind of a man he was. Maybe working for him was a good idea.

'Will you accept the job with Ross?'

'I don't know. I've told him I'd think about it. I . . . can't seem to make up my mind. I don't suppose it matters much what sort of work I do and this export business sounds interesting. I just wonder if I *should* do it. Somehow it seems to be taking advantage of Ross's kindness to me. I always seem to be on the taking end, these days. I never have anything to give him.'

'He hasn't made any conditions?' Mary asked cautiously.

'Of course not! What kind of a man do you think he is? *I'll give you a decent job if you'll go to bed with me once in a while!* I can't think of anything less likely coming from him.'

Mary shrugged.

'Obviously you've a high opinion of him, but then you always were ridiculously trusting and gullible. I know men — probably a good deal better than you do. Most things they do have a motive behind them and the motive is always to their benefit. Joe is never nicer to me than when he wants something from me whether it's sex or anything else. If Ross Bryant is falling over himself to please you, then you should at least ask yourself *why*.'

'Maybe he's just short of secretaries!' Sue said, pulling a face at her sister. She felt a trifle guilty and couldn't bring herself to tell Mary that Ross was in love with her. She wasn't even sure she believed it herself, or wanted to. He had not referred to his feelings for her since that day at Cap Estel. But when they met, everything he did was full of thought for her. He was not only attentive but sensitive to her every mood. It was the complete reversal of her life with Paul. With him, she had been the one to give all the time. She had made endless sacrifices, more than willingly, for Paul; thought up endless little surprises and ways of pleasing him; given him so many gifts, paid so many compliments. It was always his needs she had anticipated and tried to satisfy. It had been her pleasure to deny herself for him. Now with Ross, the positions were reversed. She was so unused to being on the receiving end that she was permanently being surprised and grateful.

Ross noticed this.

'One of the greatest pleasures I have is in

doing little things for you. You are always so appreciative, Sue. You take nothing, however small, for granted.'

Maybe Mary was right. There was a danger of Ross catching her on the rebound. Certainly his thoughtfulness and consideration for her had endeared him to her in a way she would not have believed possible a few weeks ago. Her feelings toward him were no longer wholly passive. She felt a genuine desire to give him something; to let him know that he had become quite important to her, even if she could not love him. She felt the need to defend him when Mary ran him down. She even wanted Mary to like him. If she went on like this, she knew she might find herself transferring her emotional needs from Paul to Ross, because it was the easiest thing to do. Ross wanted to take care of her, to love her. It wouldn't be difficult to shrug her shoulders and say: '*Why not!*'

Once Paul had said to her: 'All a man really needs from his woman is sex. If he has all he wants of that, he can do without romantic love.' If Paul was right, and she'd tried so hard to prove him wrong, then handing herself over to Ross would be simple. Paul had her heart, her deeper love; why shouldn't Ross have her body?

Oh, Sue! she reprimanded herself sharply.

Where have your ideals gone? Or, as Mary would say, your standards!

Her thoughts raced on, recalling that night with Ross. She had not once felt guilty about it. She had been so emotionally detached, she had looked back on it in almost a masculine way. Yet she could not forget his gentleness, his restraint and finally the strength of his passion. It had mastered her, disproving her belief that she would remain remote and uncaring; absorbed her to such an extent that she had forgotten Paul.

Remembering the occasion, here in her own bedroom while her sister sat silent and anxious, Sue felt the first flicker of desire for a repetition of that night.

Ross had kissed her since, on several occasions, but never made the slightest attempt to take things further. Not that he had been able entirely to conceal from her the fact that he wanted her.

As they danced he would relax his guard, draw her close against him, rest his cheek against hers, then suddenly draw quickly away from her as though he could not trust himself so close. His kisses, too, had become more ardent than intended for he would break away, his face taut and strained, and with some excuse, bid her a hurried goodnight and see her into the lift.

He never went upstairs in the lift with her.

She'd been grateful, but now today, she regretted — even resented — his self-control. She had had enough of half-heartedness from Paul. If she was ever to forget her need of him, it could only be through her intimacy with a man who wanted her so passionately, so intensely, that he was willing to throw the whole world on one side for her sake! Was Ross Bryant such a man? She doubted it. He was too diffident — too unsure of himself; too conscious of the gap in their backgrounds.

'Maybe you're right, Mary!' Sue said, her voice hardening. 'Maybe I won't take the job or see Ross once we get back to England. I might ask you to talk Joe into bringing home a few of his colleagues, eminently eligible.' She laughed stridently. 'The kind from which I can choose a suitable husband.'

Mary got up and laid an affectionate hand on her sister's shoulder.

'Darling, try not to be so bitter. It just doesn't suit you. You're still young and beautiful and dozens of men will fall in love with you, I assure you.'

'Hmm,' said Sue. 'But there won't be dozens of men I shall fall in love with. That's the real problem, Mary. I don't even want to fall in love again. If ever I feel it happening, I shall fight against it. Being in love is hell on earth. Some of it may be heaven, but most of it is hell. Maybe that's why I like Ross Bryant — I can't imagine getting into such a state over him that I felt dependent upon his smile, his approval of the clothes I buy, or the things I say, or the way I look at seven in the morning after a night of passion. Neither should I wait in for his 'phone call or die if he didn't ring. No, *no love* like that for me, ever again, Mary. If I marry, and it's a big 'if' — it'll be to a man I like and respect and who can keep me in comfort. C'*est tout!*'

Mary gave a deep sigh. It was only natural Sue should feel like this now. But it wasn't the real Sue, who was the reverse of mercenary and hard. Sooner or later, her fundamental nature would reassert itself. As Joe said, the poor girl needed a bit of time. Joe also said that Paul wasn't entirely to blame anyway. Anyone but Sue must have seen years ago which way the wind was blowing; guessed after the first year that Paul was reluctant to get that divorce. Sue ought to have known that a lover who is reluctant in the first year is hardly likely to become less so in the second, third or fourth!

Sue had blinded herself to the truth because she had never wanted to face consequences. Strange, when she was such an advocate for honesty.

In a way, Mary could understand. Women were so much more dependent on love than men. If an affair went wrong for a man, there was always his work to engross him; help him forget. But for a woman in love, her lover was her life. It was one thing to face life without him if he quit; quite another to force oneself to be the first to cut adrift. Mary, herself, had been weak over her Joe when it came to the testing point. The first act of infidelity had seemed pardonable, but a great deal harder to forgive the second time. On the third occasion her pride had demanded she leave him, but what had really happened? She'd stayed with Joe, just as Sue had stayed with Paul, hoping there wouldn't be another time; that things would get better.

As far as she knew, things *were* better between her and Joe. They were good friends. There hadn't been a girl for nearly a year. And if she did find there was another one, she'd probably forgive him again because she wouldn't be able to contemplate a life without him. One went on loving a man whatever he did. He was her husband and she had to take him as he was.

She stood up and smiled down at her sister.

'Maybe you're right, darling. We'd all be better *out* of love rather than in it. Anyway, at least it's something to see you smile. I take it you're not dining with Joe and me tonight?'

Sue bit her lip.

'I know it's our last night in La Napoule, Mary, and I feel a bit guilty about you and Joe — you've both been so marvellous to me. But Ross begged me to spend the evening with him and I hoped you'd understand . . . No, that's not quite true — I hoped that you might decide we could all at least have dinner together . . . if you'd only accept him for what he is.'

Mary drew back, some of her softness obscured again.

'Look, there's no need to feel guilty, Sue. Joe and I fully expected you'd go out with Ross Bryant and we planned a night at the Casino for ourselves. It's not that I don't want to be friendly with any friend of yours, but Ross Bryant just isn't my type. I don't suppose I'm his either, come to that. I'm sure he would rather have you to himself. It's best if we split up. After all, the holiday is over so there's little point in me trying to establish a friendship with him at this stage, is there?'

'No, I suppose not,' Sue agreed.

But after Mary had gone, she felt curiously let-down. Mary couldn't help her attitude to life and if she was being snobbish about Ross, it was probably best if they did not spend

68

their last night as a foursome. All the same, she had tentatively told Ross they might all get together. Now he'd be bound to guess the real reason for Mary's refusal and feel snubbed. The last thing Sue wanted was to hurt his feelings — though he himself had said often enough that he was well used to it. He had developed a hard shell, he'd said. Sue knew better. She knew he was vulnerable.

It's a shame, she told herself as she picked up her coat and put it round her shoulders. It's really only his voice that gives him away. If he'd been born in South Africa or Canada or Australia no one would have concerned themselves about his background. He dressed well, his manners were faultless and he'd been long enough amongst people of substance to acquire his etiquette and could take his place with the best of them. Yet people like Mary would never accept Ross Bryant or any other 'nouveau riche' except on the most casual terms — certainly never at her own conventional dinner table.

Yet I've accepted him! Sue thought with surprise.

The lift stopped and the door opened. Ross stood waiting for her. At the sound of the door opening, his head swung round and seeing her, his face lit up with pleasure.

'There you are, Sue!' he said moving

forward quickly to take her arm. 'You look gorgeous. Tonight, every man who sees you will envy me.'

He had liked her in the black chiffon dress she had worn at their first meeting, but this evening she looked beautiful and feminine in a white dress with a waistcoat embroidered with white sequins. They sparkled like the small diamonds in her ears as she moved. She carried a jade green satin bag with a diamanté clasp. She *looked* South of France, he thought. She looked a princess, everything that he had ever wanted a woman — his woman — to be.

She laughed as he led her towards the bar.

'I think you get your compliments out of a book!' she teased. 'They're much too good to be true!'

'That's because they come from the heart!' Ross said. 'I daresay I sound a bit corny but I mean all I say.' His voice was serious, but there was humour in his eyes.

He ordered her the usual martini then raised his glass and touched hers.

'To the girl I love!' he said softly, and this time, there was no possible doubt that he meant exactly what he said — words Paul had once used; words spoken with the same intensity, and conviction; words she had once believed but which, in the end, had proved meaningless.

Tears pricked her eyelids, touched her lashes but did not fall. Seeing them, Ross held tightly on to her fingers. Slowly, beneath the warm pressure of his big hand, Paul's ghost receded and she was able to smile again.

4

She sat at the table in the window, buttering toast and spreading it carefully with marmalade. It was her third piece.

Ross put his coffee cup on the bedside table. He watched her eating with a strange feeling of resentment.

If she can eat breakfast like that on top of a night like last night, she'll end up by putting on weight and losing her figure, he told himself. Not that she was in danger of it at the moment — she was too thin. If she grew plump he would no longer desire her and he would be free of this consuming need of her.

He turned his head away from the girl at the window and stared up at the ceiling, scowling. How could she eat anything at all? The long, long hours of passionate love-making had played havoc with his own nervous system; he felt tired, no, exhausted, wanted nothing at all except coffee. The dry stickiness of his throat nauseated him. He didn't even want Sue . . . although last night he had wondered if he could ever have enough of her.

She remained a complete enigma to him.

Some sixth sense told him that beneath the armour in which she encased herself, she was unusually passionate, sensuous, even; that sex could be a delight for her, too.

The frigidity on that first night was entirely mental. She had proved that to him last night, but he did not know what had happened to make her let down the barrier; to become her real self. And the adventure they had embarked on and shared had been fantastically, almost fiercely rapturous. He had not known any woman could be so desirable or that he could love as he had loved Sue through the long nocturnal hours. But then he had never made love to a woman he loved before — only to women he had desired and that, he had discovered, was an entirely different thing. He had not seemed to be able to have enough of Sue. If he wasn't making love to her, he was caressing her beautiful body, kissing her soft mouth — that incredible, soft, soft mouth. He had explored every inch of her, discovering her, wanting to touch her, run his hands over her satin-smooth skin; then retraced the rounded contours all over again.

It had been a mad, wild, exciting, wonderful night. Not the least wonderful part was that Sue had volunteered to stay with him until morning. More than that, she had begged him to let her stay with him.

'There's only an hour or two left!' she had whispered. 'Let me stay, Ross. I don't want to go back to my cold empty bed. I want to stay with you!'

Finally she had fallen asleep in his arms, her hair across her face and his, her arm flung across his chest. In the end he, too, must have slept. When they awoke, which had seemed to be in the same instant, they had made love again. Exhausted, Ross had fallen into a deeper sleep and when he woke a second time, Sue was up, wearing his white towelling bath robe, sitting by the window. The sun was pouring through the slats of the venetian blinds. She looked young, radiant, sad — so many things, he thought, and very attractive.

'I ordered breakfast to be sent up,' she said. 'I hadn't the face to order two breakfasts — I thought we'd share!'

Why should I mind how much she eats, he asked himself derisively. Really he was glad that she could. She needed to put on weight. No, what he resented was that she *wanted* to eat. He felt it could only mean last night had not affected her as it had him. *That* put him in his place! He'd do well not to forget that place, either, he told himself bitterly. Sue was still in love with that bastard, Paul. He, Ross, meant nothing but temporary consolation.

She'd made it plain a hundred times that she didn't love him. At times he had been staggered — puzzled by the wild, abandonment of their lovemaking. Now he forced himself to remember that desire and love were by no means inevitably linked. That Sue needed him as a lover in the physical sense was no indication at all that she needed him in any other way.

He was glad he felt no desire for her now as she sat there eating. It was even possible to tell himself that he didn't really need her in his life anyhow. Only two weeks ago, he'd not known of her existence. He could return to England at the end of the week and forget about her. She'd probably go back to that chap, Paul, in any event. No, he wasn't going to upset himself over Sue or any woman. He'd had his lesson years ago and this wasn't the time to forget it.

'Could I have another cup of coffee?' he asked.

She came over at once for his cup. Her smile seemed almost shy as she looked at him.

'You awake now?' she asked. 'Like some toast?'

'No, I couldn't eat a thing — thank you.'

She tilted her head to one side, looking down at him. There was no make-up on her face. Her nose was shining. He could see a tiny bruise on her throat and knew that he had made it. She looked very young — like a schoolgirl.

She didn't really understand a thing! he told himself, letting his resentment have full rein. Last night wasn't important to her. She was probably just finding out how his half of the world behaved in bed. Slumming. Lots of girls of her kind got a kick out of trying 'a bit of rough'.

'Ross?' Sue looked at him anxiously, sensing his mood had changed. He felt ashamed of his thoughts.

'Sorry, I'm probably tired!' His voice was surly.

Suddenly she bent down and kissed him, not passionately but softly on the cheek. Desire caught him without warning.

'Oh, God!' he said, and taking the cup quickly from her, pulled her down on the bed beside him and kissed her mouth. 'I thought I didn't want any more of you! What is it about you, Sue? I think I hate you. You weaken me.'

She gave a low laugh and ran her fingers through his rough hair. She did not try to release herself from his hold, nor draw her mouth away as he kissed her again and again. His seemingly inexhaustible need was comforting; so much what she needed. She wondered if he understood. *She needed his need of her*, for this alone could restore her balance — her pride — her belief in herself as a woman. Paul had taken all that from her. Ross, for a little while, was giving it back.

There had been nights like last night with Paul — but with Paul there was a difference. Such a big difference. Always *he* had withheld some innermost part of himself, as though his passion for her were on the surface.

Paul was a love with reservations. With Ross, there were none.

'You've got to marry me!' he had told her again and again as the night wore on. 'I can't live without you now. I love you. I want you. I know you don't love me but you've got to marry me all the same. I'll make you happy. Let me try, Sue, let me try. Give me a chance. I love you, darling, darling, my darling . . . '

She had lost herself in this love, this loving. His total surrender to her, his need to feel she could meet him on *his* level, had released her from the old self-made prison to which Paul alone had the key. After all, Ross had found another, more golden key. She'd finally wanted nothing but to give him what he wanted from her; and in giving it, she had discovered her own need for him.

'You don't love me, do you?' she heard his

voice, the irony encasing the hurt, the anxiety.

She brought herself quickly back to the present. She didn't want to hurt him. She felt happy and tired. She needed nothing. She would like to stay in this vacuum of 'nothingness'. But Ross wouldn't let her stay there. He pulled her out with his great consuming need, his pain and his hurt pride.

'Oh, Ross!' she whispered. She put her arms round him and pressed her face against his. 'Don't ask me for the impossible. It was such a beautiful night. Can't you be as happy this morning, as contented as I am?'

He recognised only too well what she meant. He was quick to understand — ultra sensitive to her meaning. She didn't love him. He'd never really hoped she could. He was frightened by the way the whole affair had developed. It had started as a casual interest, a physical attraction and become a tender, urgently desperate love. Now he was conscious of utter dependence upon her. With one word she could shatter him.

'I shall have to leave you soon, Ross,' she said. 'Mary said I was to be packed and downstairs by ten and it's eight-thirty now.'

'Don't go!' He hadn't meant to say more but words broke from his lips. 'Not yet, not just yet!'

This time their love-making changed again.

Now there was a quietness, a gentleness in all their caresses that was a little due to fatigue but mostly because they both knew it was also a good-bye. Neither could be sure they would ever be together again. So many things might happen to prevent their meeting in London. Neither was sure if they would want it to be this way between them even if they did see each other again.

He felt a dark cold despair. He held her as though he could not bear to let her go; as though trying to incorporate her being in his. He opened his eyes wide so that he could see her, imprint her on his memory and draw from it in his pain and loneliness later on. He knew he would never be able to feel for any other woman what he felt for Sue. And it had been for so short a time — one night in his life-time. It wasn't really fair yet there must be, he told himself, hundreds of men who never had and never would know the perfection of love.

Sue seemed to have an extra sense tuned in to him; nothing she did or said jarred on his nerves. Even now, when his sadness made him for the first time unable to express what he felt, she seemed to know. She was the leader now, kissing him, caressing every line of his strong body, repeating the discoveries of last night.

When it was over and they lay side by side, Ross said:

'It isn't going to be easy for me now — without you. But I'm not sorry, Sue. Even if I never see you again, I'm not sorry. I didn't know it was possible for love to be like this. I'm not all that young and I thought I did know most things. Perhaps we discovered nothing new, yet all of it — every little tiny part of it — was new and wonderful for me because I love you. There can't be anything more perfect than to have complete physical understanding with the woman in your arms. You are my woman, Sue . . . whether you wish it or not. I shall always feel you were created for me. And I don't just mean the sex side of it. I really love *you*, Sue. I want you to believe that.'

'Oh, Ross, I'm so sorry!'

His voice was rough as he said:

'Well, don't be. I can put up with you not loving me but I can't stand you being sorry for me. No, darling, I didn't mean that. I know what you are trying to say — that you're sorry if I've been hurt by all this. But I'm not sorry. I'm proud and grateful. Now you are going and there are to be no ties, no claims, no promises. And Sue, no goodbyes. I shan't come down and see you off. Your sister will probably think I'm rude — true to type.' He laughed without humour now. 'But I just can't watch your car drive away. I gave you my 'phone number. Maybe you'll ring me. Maybe you won't. I won't try to find you although I've no doubt I could. If you want to see me again then just ring. And if you want that job, it's open to you. Okay?'

Slowly she got off the bed and dressed. Her face was very pale and tired and troubled. She took his cup across to the table and poured him some fresh coffee.

'Afraid it's probably cold,' she said as she gave it to him. She watched him as he drank. He did not look at her.

'You aren't the only one who is grateful . . . ' she said at last, in a thick, not very steady voice. 'I am, too. Goodbye, Ross!'

When the door closed behind her, he put down the empty cup and turned on his stomach and buried his face in the pillow.

Life had not been easy for Ross Bryant and he'd taken a few knocks on his way to the top; suffered more than a few disappointments, humiliations and reverses. But they had none of them left him defeated and defenceless as the departure of this girl had done — reduced him to the point of tears.

He stayed there unmoving, unable to sleep, listening with every nerve of his body until finally, a little after ten, he heard the sound of Joe's Volvo on the road outside his window. He knew she was in it — driving away from him; knew he might never see her again.

5

It was pouring with rain. Except for the mild temperature, it might have been winter in London. The streets were dark with muddy water and although this was only the first week in July, some of the shops had lights on in their display windows.

Joe had gone to the office, Mary to the hairdressers. Sue continued her walk down the Kings Road oblivious to the state of her hair or to the ruined condition of her light suede shoes. She was as usual well dressed and her only concession to the weather was a raincoat belted round her slim waist.

Outside the block of flats she paused, her brows drawn down thoughtfully. She wasn't going into the building. She promised herself before she turned into the Kings Road that she wouldn't on any account *go in*. All she had come for was to see the place — just to test her strength of mind. Nothing more — just as a test . . .

Liar! she thought. You talk to other people about the importance of absolute truth yet you lie to yourself, kid yourself. You came here precisely at five-fifteen because that's the time Paul always arrives back from the office . . . if he's still using the flat; if he's staying the night there and not going back to the country. And you know he isn't likely to go home because it's a Thursday and midweek and Paul hates the commuters' rush.

The rain dripped off her hair and down her neck. She moved a few yards along the street into a doorway. From here she could see and not be seen. She continued her mental soliloquy.

If I'd intended to run into Paul and pretend it was an accident, I wouldn't come looking like this — waterlogged and bedraggled. So that much at least is true. I just want to *see him* — see how he's looking; find out if he's alone or if he's found someone to replace me.

She felt a little crazy, reckless and out of control. Mary would never understand. Mary had not understood what Paul's letter, awaiting her return from France, had done to her. But then she had not allowed Mary to read it. She had burnt it herself, as if it was of no importance to her. It didn't matter, of course, that she had burnt it. She knew it by heart.

'My darling Sue,
I cannot begin to tell you how much I am missing you. Someone told me you

84

were abroad with your sister and I can imagine you in the South of France, golden brown and more beautiful than ever. Remember the holiday we planned to have there together and it never materialised? So many things we planned but never did, and I know this was my fault. I can understand you feeling bitter and disillusioned but whatever you think, you must believe I love you. You can't wipe out seven years as if they had not existed. I'm missing you. I can't be strong minded about us and do what I suppose is the right thing and leave you in peace. I suppose if I were really unselfish I would want you to meet someone else, get married and enjoy a life without me. But I don't, Sue, and I can't. I beg you at least to see me again so we can talk this out. You left in such an emotional state and never gave me the chance to put my point of view. I keep on the flat hoping that you will eventually start missing me as much as I do you and realise as I do that our lives are bound together however much you might wish it otherwise.

Come back to me, Sue. You can name your own conditions. I swear I will do everything in my power to comply. Whatever kind of a bastard I may have been in the past, I've always loved and

*needed you and knowing me as well as you
do, you'll realise what it has cost me to beg
you to return to me.*

Please, Sue, please.

Your Paul'

'Utter rubbish!'

Sue could imagine that would be Mary's comment had she seen the letter. But Mary had never believed in Paul's love. Not everyone was as strong a character as Mary, Sue reminded herself. If Paul had been free when they had first met, he would have married her and they would be happily together now. It wasn't his fault they had found each other too late — after his marriage to Melanie, and that his conscience wouldn't allow him to break with her. Sue knew that he wasn't still in love with his wife. He loved *her*, Sue.

For one whole week she fought the desperate desire to answer Paul's letter. The phrase '*name your own conditions*' was so tempting. Sue could at last insist on marriage. She could make Paul begin divorce proceedings. But, of course, she'd never wanted him to divorce Melanie at her instigation. It had to be because he wanted it that way . . . and he never had. Even now he did not write: *I'm going to divorce Melanie because I need you.*

So why was she here? Just to see him. She might learn by looking at his face if he were as desperate as his letter sounded. She'd certainly find out if he returned to the flat with another girl. Then, at last, Sue would truly be free. She needed fuel for hatred, for putting an end to all that had ever been between them. If he had replaced her she would not forgive him.

Several people went into the building, shaking umbrellas and obviously glad to be out of the downpour. One or two faces were familiar, but there was no Paul. Suddenly she wondered if he could already be there; have come home early as he very occasionally did with some work he could do in peace away from the office.

She hesitated, then walked into the block. The hall porter came over to her.

'Mrs Manton, how nice to see you, Madam! And goodness me, you're soaked through. Who'd think this was July!'

'I've been abroad!' Sue said nervously. 'Mr Manton hasn't come in yet, I suppose?'

'No, Madam; at least I've not seen him. He doesn't usually get back till later — not since you've been away. He usually eats out, then comes home.'

'Yes, of course!'

The porter was moving towards the lift,

opening the door ready for her. She shook her head.

'No, I'm not going up now, Banks, thank you . . . I've some shopping to do.'

She pushed open the heavy glass doors and hurried away, knowing that he must be staring after her in some surprise. She cared and yet didn't care what he thought. She turned into the street and walked towards Sloane Square Underground, her heart beating painfully, and in time with her hurried steps. A voice inside her head kept repeating: 'Fool! Fool! Fool!'

Her journey had accomplished nothing — exactly nothing. Even if she had seen Paul and he hadn't seen her, what could it have done? His face might have been hidden behind his umbrella. It would have told her nothing. As to his having another girlfriend with him, that was Mary's way of thinking, not hers.

She sat in the train amongst the commuters, crushed together, damp, steaming. She felt flushed now with heat whereas a while ago she had been shivering. She was ashamed of her own weakness. Of course she had wanted more than just a glimpse of Paul. *Of course* she had really hoped he would recognise her, sweep her upstairs with him, over-riding her objection and then . . .

Weak, stupid idiot! she told herself, her gaze fastening on the pools of rain water gathering at her feet.

Automatically she changed trains at the right station and got onto the Hampstead tube.

Mary would be back by now, Joe soon afterwards. They'd have drinks, dinner, watch something on television, then go to bed. At least she didn't have to go back to an empty flat like some lonely people — alone with their griefs and their despair.

Sue let herself into the flat and met Mary in the hall, looking pink and chic, fresh from the hairdressers, her hair smooth and shining. Mary surveyed her young sister with dismay.

'You're absolutely soaked to the skin!' she cried. 'What on earth have you been doing?'

'Shopping!' Sue said vaguely. 'I got caught in a down-pour!'

'Well, go and have a hot bath. You'll get a chill,' Mary wailed. 'Oh, and there was a 'phone message for you.' Her voice had hardened perceptibly. The colour rushed into Sue's cheeks and her head shot up. 'Yes!' Mary went on bitingly, '*Paul*. I told him you were out and wouldn't have spoken to him if you'd been in but he said he'd ring again so you might as well be warned. I presume you don't *want* to speak to him?'

Sue tried desperately to collect her thoughts. Banks must have told Paul she'd called at the block. So he had come home at the usual time after all. If she'd only waited a little longer . . .

'Well?' Mary insisted. 'I take it you aren't going to weaken. Remember what you said to me . . . *Don't let me talk to him, Mary, no matter how much I argue — no matter what he says. Keep me away from him.*'

'Yes, I remember, and you're right, of course!' The colour drained out of Sue's face and her big, tired eyes suddenly looked as if a light had gone out inside her.

Mary said quickly, gently:

'That's my Sue. It'll get easier, darling. I do wish that brute would leave you in peace. I suppose he's finally beginning to realise he has lost you, and he's stepping up the pressure. Trust a man to begin to value something only when he thinks it's out of reach!'

'I'll go and have my bath!' Sue said and escaped into her own bedroom.

As she stripped off her wet clothes, she caught sight of herself in the mirror. She was still a golden brown from France — only a few brief pale strips left by her bikini. That holiday in La Napoule seemed an eternity away already. In ten days it was as if they'd never been away at all. She was back on the old tread-mill, taut, desperate, and emotionally as weak as ever.

She lay in the hot water with tired eyes closed and remembered Ross — that curious strange man who had managed to make her happy for two whole weeks. He didn't seem real now, anymore than did those two nights of love-making. In retrospect it was inconceivable that she could have let any other man but Paul touch her.

She tried to recapture the strange peace and contentment that had soothed and comforted her when Ross Bryant was around. He'd been so sweet, so gentle and loving. She'd been happy with him. Yet since her return to London she had barely given him a thought.

The 'phone rang insistently. She forgot Ross. *This must be Paul again.* Through the bathroom door she heard Mary's high pitched voice:

'Yes, yes, that's right. No, this is *Mary*. No — she's in the bath. Shall I call her? Yes, of course.'

Sue couldn't understand it. Mary had all but forbidden her to speak to Paul — yet she was being most accommodating with him.

'Sue? Can you hear me? You're wanted on

the 'phone. It's Ross Whatsisname — the one you met in La Napoule.'

The darkness closed in on Sue again. Hope receded. She stepped out of the bath, flung a towel round her and unlocked the door. Mary looked in.

'You remember, your holiday boyfriend!' she whispered.

Sue smiled.

'The blacksmith's grandson,' she said, knowing that was what Mary had wanted to say.

She picked up the receiver and said: 'Hullo?' At once Ross's voice with its definite accent, brought her a vivid mental picture of him.

'Sue? Hullo. I know I promised not to do this but I just had to find out how you are. Are you angry?'

'No, of course not!' But she was surprised. It was a coincidence that he should telephone her just when she had been thinking about him for the first time since they'd said goodbye. 'As a matter of fact,' she went on, 'I was thinking about our holiday just before you 'phoned. You know, seeing myself in the bath, still sun-burnt.'

'Wish I were there to see you still sun-burnt in the bath!'

Despite her earlier depression, she laughed.

'How are you, Sue? Thought any more about that job?'

'No, I haven't!' Sue said truthfully. 'I've been rather awful about getting myself some work. I really can't go on sponging off my sister. As a matter of fact, I'd planned to start haunting the agencies on Monday.'

'Well, don't! Take that job in my firm. Good pay, good staff facilities, pension, holidays, the lot, and a soft-hearted good-natured boss into the bargain.'

She laughed again.

'You've almost talked me into it. I will think about it, Ross, I promise.'

'Better still, come out and discuss it with me. I'm fully qualified to answer all your questions. Besides, I'm an excellent salesman and I'll guarantee to get myself a new secretary on the pay roll in one hour flat.'

'Don't boast!' Sue teased him.

'You mean it isn't done in the best circles?'

She laughed again.

'Well are you coming out to dinner?'

'Ross, I can't! I'd love to, but I can't.'

Some of the eager gaiety left his voice.

'Tomorrow, then?'

She hesitated. She *could* go, of course, but did she *want* to re-open their short friendship? If it meant nothing more than friendship, yes ... but they'd started at the wrong end of the road. It had begun, absurdly and quite accidentally as far as she was concerned, in bed. Only later, when they knew each other better, had they begun sincerely to like each other. After which, Ross had fallen in love with her . . . or at least, believed that he was in love.

'You don't want to see me again?' she heard him ask.

'I didn't say that. Oh, all right, Ross, tomorrow.'

'That's marvellous. When? Where?' Now his voice sounded young and eager again. 'I'll let you choose the place. Shall we do a theatre first?'

Sue felt a remembered comfort in the way he always tried so hard to please her.

'We don't exactly know what the other would enjoy in a play, do we? How about a film? I remember seeing a notice when I was in Chelsea this afternoon about a special showing of 'The Agony and the Ecstasy.' Have you ever seen it?'

'No, I haven't and I'd like to. It's about that painter. Can't remember his name. Michael someone?'

Sue drew in her breath, at first shocked at Ross's ignorance, then amused. Finally an entirely different emotion swept over her. Ross had not had the same education as herself. She ought not to forget that. Gently, she said:

'Michelangelo. The film is the story of his life. Maybe it wouldn't be very interesting now I stop to think about it.'

At once, Ross protested.

'It's exactly the kind of film I ought to see and would enjoy seeing with you. You can explain it all to me and I can't think of anyone I'd rather have as a teacher. I'm glad you suggested it. Now, where would you like to eat? Somewhere smart? Somewhere quiet?'

For a moment Sue hesitated. Then she said:

'Somewhere quiet, I think. There's a small French restaurant in Sloane Street, not too far away from the cinema. The food's good and we'd be able talk there in peace. That's if we can get a table.'

'Leave that to me. I'll fix it,' Ross said with authority in his voice.

They completed their arrangements.

Sue went back to her bath and once more relaxed in the warm water. There was no doubt about it, Ross was good for her. The appalling depression of half an hour ago was gone. She was even looking forward to tomorrow.

She wondered what Mary would say when she heard about her date. Disapprove, probably. It was as well Mary knew nothing of Ross's intellectual limitations. It was just the kind of thing Mary would seize on and bring up on every possible occasion to prove that no matter what Sue said, a gulf still existed between the well educated and the self-made man.

So what? Sue asked herself. Probably Ross knew about things of which she and Mary were ignorant. One could learn from the other. One of the most endearing things about Ross was that he didn't mind being told, or at least, he had seemed anxious to acquire the kind of culture he lacked.

Feeling warmer, and a good deal happier, Sue stepped out of the bath and dressed for dinner. Joe was home. She could hear him calling out to Mary to leave her cooking and have a drink.

When Sue finally joined them, Joe whistled appreciatively. She looked beautiful in a straight blue, wild silk dress edged with satin.

'That colour certainly suits you, Sue. You look fabulous. Been to the hairdresser with Mary?'

'Joe's right — you do look nice, darling,' Mary said. 'What did your boyfriend want, by the way?'

'He wants me to go out tomorrow evening. I've said I will.'

Mary frowned.

'Oh dear, I thought you weren't going to go on seeing him,' she began, but Joe interrupted.

'The girl's got to go out with someone occasionally, Mary. Besides, if the fellow cheers her up and his 'phone call seems to have done the trick, then I'd say he makes a good tonic for her.'

The telephone rang, disturbing them and preventing Mary arguing the matter further. With a swift look at Sue, she hurried out of the sitting room into the hall. Sue's hand tightened round her sherry glass, the knuckles showing white. Her gaze followed Mary through the door. This must be Paul.

She heard Mary's cold curt voice:

'No, she doesn't wish to speak to you or to see you. No, I'm sorry, Paul, but that's exactly what she told me to tell you. No!'

She came back into the room, her eyes sparkling dangerously.

'Damn that man!' she exploded. 'Accused me of interfering in your life, Sue; said I was responsible for a lot of trouble by not minding my own business. He seemed to think I'm forcibly preventing you from answering the 'phone.'

Joe grinned at his sister-in-law — a sympathetic grin.

'Not far wrong, eh, Sue?'

She tried to smile but it faded out. She couldn't answer Joe. She sat silent, confused, loathing her own weakness. Her heart was pounding.

'Oh, well, dinner will be burnt to a cinder!' Mary said sighing. 'Come on, you two, drink up — let's go and have our meal. I want to watch the play on the box tonight.'

Sue had no appetite, although the chile con carne Mary had made was very good. Her stomach felt as though it were a tight, hard knot. She was all too familiar with this symptom of her tension. When she was upset it was as though an invisible hand suddenly pulled the strings tightly together in her solar plexus and the result was agonising.

Joe and Mary started to argue about a play they had both watched on television. Sue's thoughts were far away. Maybe if she could slip out of the flat later, during the play, she might find a 'phone box nearby and ring Paul. But no, that would be weak and futile. Mary was right. It would do no good, talking to him. Everything there was to say had already been said. Paul had had his chance . . . seven years of chances in fact, to get his freedom and hadn't done so. That was why she had left him . . .

98

'For the ninth time, Sue, have you finished?'

Biting her lip, Sue looked down at her half empty plate and nodded. She spoke apologetically:

'It's delicious, Mary, but I suppose I'm a bit tired . . . '

'Nonsense!' Mary interrupted. 'What you mean is, that 'phone call from Paul Manton has ruined your appetite. One of these days someone is going to find that man dead in bed and you, Joe, will be hiring a first-rate counsel in order to save your wife from a life sentence!'

'Wouldn't come as a surprise,' Joe commented. 'You've certainly said enough to be convicted as a suspect. Can't we forget our Mr Manton for a moment? I'm getting fed up with hearing his name.'

Mary opened her mouth to argue with him, her cheeks flushed. She looked ready for battle. Quickly, Sue intervened.

'Joe's quite right. Let's forget Paul. Please, Mary?'

Conversation veered round to Ross. Joe started to tease Sue about 'her boyfriend'. He gave the impression that he sympathised with her. He was a good natured man, thought Sue, but she found it difficult to keep up the kind of repartee he enjoyed. She made the effort because she felt guilty about Joe. Not every brother-in-law would be as ready as he to have her staying here for so long, a permanent third, when he was used to being alone with Mary. Moreover, Joe bore the brunt of the expense although Sue's father had been generous and sent her a small allowance after she left Paul. At first, she had not touched it, pride forbidding her to accept anything from the father with whom she had never been reconciled. Then — more for Mary's and Joe's sake — she began to draw on it. It had been necessary before going to France, in order to buy clothes and have something to spend during her holiday. She must now get a job — that seemed essential. On Monday, without fail, she would apply to a good secretarial agency and find something she would like. Her shorthand might be rusty but she could soon regain her speed with practice.

Lying in bed later that night, Sue thought again about Ross's offer of a job. In a way, it would be nice starting work where at least she knew someone and wouldn't be the complete new girl! Like going to a new school, bearable and even a little exciting if one knew even one other person there. But of course if she went to work for him, she wouldn't allow Ross to give her preferential treatment. That much she would make clear at the beginning. She'd work the same hours, accept the same wages, as the rest of the girls.

But she could not keep her mind on Ross for long. It kept straying. Soon she was back on the familiar treadmill fighting against the deep-rooted desire to see Paul again . . . just to see him, if nothing more . . . just to hear what he had to say . . . just to find out if, after all, he might be contemplating a divorce . . . just . . .

Finally she slept.

6

Ross held her hand throughout the film. There had been no argument about it — he'd simply taken her hand as the film started, and continued to hold it tightly in his own. Otherwise, his complete attention was on the screen.

Sue at first felt very conscious of him. When he'd called at the flat, she was a little surprised to find how much a stranger he seemed. The smart grey suit was totally unfamiliar. She'd only seen him in shorts and beach clothes or dark trousers with a Continental white jacket. Also she had forgotten how tall — how large he was. In Mary's small Hampstead flat, he had seemed to fill the room.

Joe was still at work but Mary was home, bristling a little but her natural good manners preventing her from being anything but polite. Over-polite, Sue thought grimly, as they all three exchanged greetings.

She herself had felt nervous, uneasy, although she knew she looked good. Her hair was smooth and shining and she wore the blue dress Joe liked. She knew it suited her.

She had put on her make-up with extra care but those dark shadows under her eyes could not quite be obliterated.

'So you aren't tied to office hours?' Mary was asking, her voice brittle and faintly critical. 'Poor Joe can't get away like this. You're lucky.'

Ross's reply was apologetic.

'Well, being the 'boss' so to speak, I come and go as I please. Sue said she didn't want too late a night so we decided on the early programme. Then we can dine at eight-thirty.'

Sue was more conscious of Ross's accent here than she had been in France. Not that it was more marked; probably she was just hypersensitive to Mary's criticism. She heard him with Mary's ears. It was stupid and she knew it. In France, his accent had become so familiar she'd taken it in her stride.

But in the taxi taking them to Chelsea they had turned and smiled at each other and both seemed to relax. Ross said:

'It *is* lovely to be with you again. You look very beautiful. You always do. Now tell me I'm wearing rose-coloured specs. I know it embarrasses you if I pay you compliments.'

Sue laughed.

'I suppose if I were an American, I'd say casually: 'Why, thank you!' as though I were used to being told how beautiful I am every day of the week. I just don't seem to have that kind of sophistication, or is it self-confidence?'

'I'm glad you're not American. I like your soft English voice. I could listen to you talking for hours. Sometimes women in your set talk far too loudly — you can hear them shouting *Darleeeng* at each other in restaurants! But you have a soft voice. Now I'll shut up and give you a chance to talk to me. Tell me more about Michelangelo, your great Italian painter and, presumably, the Great Lover, too!'

She smiled.

'Well, not exactly. As a matter of fact, he was a homosexual. That's probably why most of his paintings are of beautiful boys like David, rather than of girls. He wasn't the kind of man you probably imagine. There was nothing effeminate about him. He was a strong, virile person. His work on the Sistine Chapel roof required colossal physical strength and endurance.'

Ross grunted.

'Always seems such a terrible waste of a life when a man is that way. I can't understand how it happens, although of course I know the usual explanations. But I still don't really understand.'

'That's because you yourself are so

104

essentially masculine!' Sue said. 'Perhaps if you'd been different, the kind of experience you had as a young boy might have turned even you against women.'

Ross grinned.

'Far from it. For some years I took every and any girl who'd have me. Trying to prove I wasn't what that first one thought I was, I suppose, and probably proved she was right! Then I quietened down and became more selective.'

Remembering their conversation, Sue thought how extraordinary it was that they could talk about intimate things so easily and naturally, as though they had been friends for years. Ross seemed to jump straight past all the preliminaries of friendship, carrying her with him onto a different plane. Even the way he had just taken hold of her hand obviously not intending to let it go, fascinated her. He was so very different from Paul.

Then the film claimed her attention and she didn't become aware of Ross again until it was over and he was leading her out into the bright lights of the foyer.

'You didn't want to stay for the second film, did you?' he asked as if he already knew her answer. 'I think it would have been quite an anti-climax. I'm so glad you made me see 'The Agony and the Ecstasy', Sue. It was magnificent and very interesting.'

They continued to discuss the film as they dined at the French restaurant. He had managed to secure a corner table which was as secluded as possible. He had already ordered the meal and with it, an iced hock which brought back memories of France and set them both laughing.

'I never drink champagne now without remembering what you told me!' he said. 'I want you always to tell me when I don't do things the way they should be done. Promise, Sue? However much it might embarrass you or me?'

He watched her expression; he felt that he would never tire of looking at her; at that lovely face — the eyes at first shy, then frank and friendly. He loved her more than he'd done in France, he thought. That last week without her had been hell. Finally he'd caught an earlier plane back to London, unable to bear La Napoule without her. But in London he'd felt even more strangely bereft. Everywhere he went — and he plunged into work, anxious to be as busy as possible — he kept wondering if he would run into her. He'd promised he would not 'phone her, but lost the battle. In the end he'd had to get his secretary to look up Joe's number and from then on, it was only a matter of time, before he'd lifted the receiver.

Now he was happy — or if not entirely happy, at least less restless and disturbed. Sue was with him. He didn't like the look of fatigue, of strain which had returned to her face; nor the sad troubled look in her eyes. She'd lost that for a while in France. He felt challenged to bring back the laughter — the radiance that could shine like an inner light as she smiled.

She was smiling at him now but suddenly, her whole body stiffened. Her face paled and she gave a gasp.

'What's the matter, Sue? Are you ill?'

He leaned across the table anxiously.

'Get me out of here, Ross, please, quickly. I want to leave. At once!'

They had not yet quite finished their first course. He thought of the orange sorbet she'd remarked on at Cap Estel and which he had ordered the head waiter to prepare especially this evening as a surprise for her. But he said nothing. He beckoned to the man and pulled some notes from his wallet.

'This should cover everything!' he said and stood up to help Sue into her coat. As he touched her shoulders, he was shocked by her violent trembling. She looked quite ill. He put an arm round her and they walked together out of the restaurant. An empty taxi came along. Ross darted forward and stopped it.

'Where to?'

'The Dorchester!' Ross replied and stepped in beside Sue. At once, she turned to him and he put his arms round her.

'I'm s . . . so . . . sorry!' she gasped. Her teeth were chattering as if from cold. Her hands were cold. 'Please, Ross, please believe me. I'm sorry.'

He drew a deep breath.

'I can't say I understand, but no matter. Are you ill? What has happened, darling?' The endearment slipped out. Suddenly, she was in tears; deep shuddering sobs rent her. They really frightened him. Not knowing what else to do, he held her tightly in his arms; thankful, for once, for the usual endless traffic jams holding up the taxi's route to the hotel.

Within minutes she had calmed down. She borrowed Ross's handkerchief and dabbed her eyes.

'I must look a sight!' she said in a small shaky voice. She took out a compact from her handbag and powdered her nose before outlining her mouth with lipstick.

'Want to talk about it now?' he asked, watching her with tender concern.

'Ross . . . I can't discuss it. I might cry again. Perhaps you'd better take me home.'

'I have a suite at the Dorchester,' Ross

broke in with a calm he was not exactly feeling. 'It's a bedroom and sitting room so we can go up there, have a drink, and get you sorted out. Okay?'

She nodded helplessly.

Ross leaned back in the taxi, holding her closer. He was deliberately talkative.

'I don't ordinarily live at the Dorchester although I suppose it would be an impressive address. As a matter of fact, the lease of my old flat in Chelsea expired and I decided not to renew it — thought I'd prefer to live this way. Or at least, be near the Parks. I'm country born and bred and I need trees. You never feel the lack of trees in London, Sue? Not that you do too badly in Hampstead . . . '

He talked on until they arrived at the hotel. Ross gave her his key and told her to go on ahead of him; he wanted to order coffee, some sandwiches and fresh fruit. He saw her into the lift.

She let herself into the small entrance and then into the sitting room, and was duly impressed by the beauty and elegance of it. Of course she had heard that one of the suites in this hotel cost more for a week than many families spent on food for a month. It struck her suddenly how many people argued that it was unfair that the rich should be able to 'waste money' while the poor struggled. Mary felt that way. They had been arguing about it only the other night. But Joe had sided with Sue who had always been of the opinion that there would always be some who had the brains to make more money than others.

Ross had started with nothing and all this money he was now spending had been produced through his personal efforts. Sue saw absolutely no reason to begrudge him his luxury living.

She was ready to admit that she, too, enjoyed the good things. She appreciated the beautiful colouring of walls and carpets; the concealed lights; the gorgeous curtains; the light streaming through the delicate net curtains. Pushing them aside, she could see the park and a long stream of cars below in Park Lane.

This was the heart of London. Here, the millionaires lived. Was Ross moving in that direction?

There were all the latest magazines and newspapers on the round glass table in front of the brocade sofa. She saw a box of cigars; pink carnations in a vase on the desk where there was also headed notepaper ready for the occupant. Moved by curiosity, she glanced into the bedroom; perfectly furnished, all very neat and tidy. On the dressing chest she could see ivory-backed brushes with the initials

'R.B.', a bottle of expensive aftershave, and an alarm clock.

On the table by the bed were two books. Curious to know what Ross was reading, she glanced at them swiftly and moved back into the sitting room with a slight smile on her lips.

One title had been 'Taste in Literature'. The other, 'Modern Art'. She was touched, positive that until Ross had met her he had never bothered about art or literature. Some of the bitterness, the acute misery about Paul lessened.

Then Ross came into the room.

'All right?' he asked. 'I've ordered coffee and a bottle of brandy. I think you need a strong drink, Sue.'

She sat down on the sofa and nervously flicked through a magazine.

'I want to apologise properly for having spoiled your evening and robbed you of your dinner.'

He sat down beside her.

'That's okay — I've ordered smoked salmon and chicken, in case you re-find your appetite. Last time we had a meal together you were fairly tucking in — remember? It was breakfast at our hotel in my room. I was very irritated because you had such an appetite.'

He had successfully managed to divert her attention if only for a few moments.

'Irritated, Ross? But why?'

He laughed.

'Because I'm sentimental at heart. I looked upon your hunger as a sure sign you weren't in love with me. I was really more hurt than annoyed.'

There was a knock at the door. A waiter came in with a big tray which he put down on the table between them. After he had gone, Ross handed Sue her brandy.

'Now!' he said, his eyes no longer smiling. 'If you'd like to, will you tell me what happened in the restaurant?'

Sue stared into her glass. Her colour was returning. It was a warm night. The net curtains blew in from the open windows. She drew a deep breath.

'I'm afraid you are going to find it hard to forgive me, Ross. I've been thoughtless and . . . ' she looked up suddenly, her eyes full of appeal ' . . . I shan't blame you for what you'll think about me, but you must believe I'm sorry.' She looked away again, unnerved by the steady way his eyes held hers. He was frowning a little, in an effort to understand what it was all about.

'Confession coming up. That restaurant we went to was one Paul and I used to go to

112

often. He came in tonight. I suppose that's just what I was hoping would happen, yet when it did I couldn't face him. No, that's not quite true. I didn't *plan* it that way, Ross. You told me to suggest a place to eat and that one jumped to mind as being fairly near the cinema. It was only after you'd rung off I realised we *might* run into Paul. I told myself it was unlikely — too much of a coincidence he'd be there the same evening we were, and even if he were, it wouldn't matter. That's when I should have known better, Ross. I didn't allow myself to dwell on the possibility of running into Paul because I didn't want to cancel our plans. Now I've ruined our whole evening and I feel terrible about it, honestly.'

He heard her out in silence. He did not try to hide the fact that he was very much shaken by what she had told him. He was shocked to find she was still so deeply involved with this man, Paul, that the sight of him could affect her so violently as to make her physically ill. He was hurt, too, that she had cared so little about their evening together that she would risk it being spoiled. He was also suddenly doubtful as to whether or not she had been using him as a means of seeing Paul again; that despite her denial, the choice of restaurant was deliberate.

He did not know what to say to her. At this

moment, he was both hating and loving her. He wanted to be able to tell her to get out and go home and leave him in peace; yet he wanted also to keep her here with him always; to prove she didn't need this other man who seemed to have such an extraordinary hold over her.

'I'm very much ashamed of myself!' Sue said quietly. She put down her brandy and stood up. 'Now I think I'd better go home. You certainly won't want me to stay.'

'I don't think you know very much about anything!' Ross interrupted her. 'I think you're reacting in a completely overemotional manner without using a grain of logic or common sense. What you need is to face facts once and for all.'

She stood there hesitantly, looking down at him.

'You can't hope to master your problems by running away from them!' Ross went on, still not looking at her. 'I learned that years ago. Let's forget the question of whether or not you ran into Paul deliberately; it doesn't affect your reaction. Why did you run away? What did you think he could do to you, there and then, in the middle of a restaurant? Are you physically afraid of him?'

She shook her head and sat down weakly in her chair.

'No, of *course* not. I'm not really afraid of him at all. I'm afraid of myself, Ross. I know I'm weak. I know I'm far too emotional. I know how completely I'm tied to Paul, emotionally tied. I still love him, Ross. He wants me back and I suppose eventually I'll end up with him again. I'm fighting it but deep down I know it isn't much use. Sooner or later I'll give in. I can't help myself.'

'If you do, it will be over my dead body!' Ross said with unexpected violence. His face was hot — his eyes sparkling dangerously. Then, surprisingly, he smiled. 'I know, you'll tell me this has nothing to do with me; I'm a stranger in your life, without substance or importance. But whether you want it or not, Sue, I'm your *friend* and a real one. I simply can't stand by and see you going back to Paul; living with a man who cannot really love you however much you try to kid yourself he does.'

'You sound like Mary!' Sue said. Then she added: 'The trouble is I know you are right; I know Mary is right; I know I did the right thing to leave him, but that doesn't stop me wishing that I hadn't.'

'You were happy with him then?'

She shook her head. He could read the pain and despair in her eyes and if there was any man he hated it was Paul Manton.

'No, I don't suppose I was, but I belong to him, Ross. I don't see how any girl could live with a man, share his life, be part of him for seven years and not become as tied to him as though they were married.'

'You're really telling me he's a habit — like smoking; a habit as difficult to break. But it can be done, Sue. After all, plenty of married couples who were together a good deal longer than you and Paul have been divorced or lost their partner through death yet found someone else.'

Sue shrugged her shoulders.

'I'm not so blind to Paul's faults as to think there doesn't exist a better man somewhere in the world . . . maybe even one I could learn to love. But it's Paul I love and want now. He wrote to me while I was abroad. He wants me back. He says I can name my conditions.'

The man listening to her moved suddenly and his lips tightened. He gave her a searching look.

'You mean, he'd be willing to get a divorce and marry you?'

She was honest enough not to lie.

'I'm not sure of that. He didn't *say* so. I suppose it *might* drift back to the way it was — saying yes, he'll get a divorce, then putting it off and off and off. Oh, God, I don't know, Ross. I'm beginning to wonder if I really care if he'd marry me or not.'

'Of course you care!' Ross spoke fiercely, furiously. 'You care, if not for conventional reasons, then because you aren't the kind of girl who wants to share her man; and because you know deep down inside that if he really loved you, he'd offer you nothing less than marriage and security.'

She sat silent — agonised. He saw the agony.

He looked at her white, troubled face and felt a hot stab of jealousy, so violent that he had to pour himself another brandy and drink it down. His thoughts steadied. Then Sue reached out a hand and touched his arm and at the contact, he at once experienced a sense of hope — of joy that preceded an intense wave of desire for her. Memories of the nights he had held her in his arms, loving her with all the ecstasy of her responsiveness, her kisses — the urgency of his need to take her in his arms again became unbearable.

The strength of his own feelings shocked him. He was unnerved to realise that a mere touch from her could evoke such powerful reactions. Deliberately he refrained from covering her hand with his own. If he allowed his iron control to snap he knew in seconds he would make love to her. Yet she seemed unaware of his feelings. In that soft voice that he found so irresistible, she was pleading with him.

'Tell me what to do. I know you are right, but I can't go on fighting this thing alone. Help me, please. Mary seems to think time is all I need, but time will be my undoing. The longer it goes on the weaker I seem to feel.'

With a great effort he kept apart from her, but his whole body was shaking.

'Then we must see you do not have too much time on your hands,' he said. 'Take that job I've been holding open for you, Sue. That's the first move. Then agree to come out with me as often as I ask you — which I can promise will be very often.'

Sue looked at him dubiously.

'You mean you still want to go on seeing me — after the way I've behaved this evening?'

He nodded. Suddenly he was angry with her because she would not accept the fact that he was in love with her; as much in love with her as she was with Paul. She need not imagine she had a monopoly on love, he thought with all the pent up passion of body and mind. He stood up. He almost glared at her.

'Come, I'll take you home,' he said roughly. 'You look dead beat. A good night's sleep will put some colour back in your cheeks before

118

we meet for lunch tomorrow. And don't refuse. I'll expect you here at one-thirty. Okay?'

She nodded her assent.

But once in the taxi he could no longer take refuge in anger. He felt protective, compassionate toward her as she leaned her cheek against his shoulder. He buried his lips in her hair and held her with a new fierce possessiveness. Paul Manton would not take her away from him; nor would he ever permit her to go back to him. Whether she liked it or not, she was going to be his.

But his confidence was short-lived. All too soon followed the uncomfortable thought that because of her background and his, he could not contemplate Sue ever agreeing to become his wife.

7

The next morning the 'phone rang twice. The first time it was Ross renewing the invitation to lunch and naming time and place. Mary, on her way out to the shops, eyed Sue significantly.

'Dead keen, isn't he? Watch your step, sister mine, or you'll be in another fine old mess.'

Sue flung back her head defiantly.

'Ross is nice — *very* nice, and I'll see as much of him as I want.'

Mary shrugged her shoulders.

'It's your business. All the same, I should have thought you could do better with a more educated type.'

'Not that *again*!' Sue said wearily.

With another shrug, Mary departed through the front door.

Ten minutes later the 'phone rang a second time. It was Paul. As she heard his voice, Sue felt such a tightness in her throat she could hardly speak.

'Hello? Hello?' repeated Paul.

'Oh, it's you!' she said stupidly. 'I thought it was . . .'

'That man I saw you with at Marcels last

night? Who is he? Why did you rush off in such a hurry?'

Paul's voice sounded jealous. It was a slow, rich, cultured voice; bitterly familiar.

She felt suddenly steadier. Calmly she said:

'He was just a friend. I met him abroad. I didn't notice *you* in the restaurant!' The lie tripped out easily.

'You sound very cool. Didn't you get my letter? Are you still determined to keep up this stupid quarrel?'

She caught her breath. Of all the understatements!

'Yes, I got the letter. But there really doesn't seem to me to be any point in starting up again. I wish you'd stop writing or 'phoning, Paul.'

There was a pause, in which Sue felt her nerves quivering like taut wires. Then Paul said:

'Banks said you were round at the flat. You were, weren't you, Sue? Why didn't you come in? Didn't you want to see me? Are you afraid of me?'

Yes, damn you, I am! Sue thought. But aloud she said:

'How silly — of course not! I just don't see any point in our meeting Paul. It's all over between us.'

'Well, I do. For one thing, you've been very

unfair to me, darling. You never did give me a chance to state my side of the picture. You never warned me you were walking out on me. How do you think I felt getting back that night and finding you gone? It was a pretty cowardly way to break things off — after *seven* years, Sue.'

She watched two dark red petals drift from a great bunch of roses arranged on the hall table.

She picked up the petals and crushed them in her hand.

'Maybe seven years was too long for me, Paul. Anyway, it's over now and . . . '

'It's not over for me. I still love you, Sue. I've missed you desperately. It's been hell without you. I've nearly gone out of my mind asking myself *why*? Where did I go wrong?'

'Don't be stupid, Paul!' Sue surprised herself as she heard her own cool, remote voice. 'You know perfectly well why I went.'

'Well, there's no point 'jobbing backwards' as one of my stockbroker friends is always saying. The point is now to try and put things right. You've got to come back to me, Sue. I need you desperately. I'll do anything you want, only you *must* come back.'

He sounded genuine. His insistent voice surprised her and caught at her heart-strings. She felt that she was weakening.

'Please, Paul. I don't want to.'

'You mean you don't love me any more?'

'I didn't say that. I just said I don't intend to come back. I don't want to. It's no use, Paul. You don't really want to divorce Melanie and I shall not ask you to. It's as simple as that.'

She could hear Paul striking a match and lighting a cigarette; could hear his indrawn breath as he inhaled. Obviously, he was not afraid she would ring off. He had sensed that she was vacillating.

'Supposing I'm willing to divorce Melanie? To set things going right away? What then?'

'I'm tired of supposing that,' Sue hardened. 'I've heard it too often, Paul. From now on, there will be no married man in my life.'

'So the man you were with last night isn't married?'

Sue could almost see Paul frown. He used to wrinkle his forehead and shut his eyes when something annoyed or hurt him.

'No, he's not.'

'You don't mind hitting below the belt, do you, Sue! I suppose I can't blame you for wanting to hurt me. You're quite right, of course. I did promise to get divorced and I broke that promise but you knew it wasn't my fault. Do you think if I'd met you first there'd ever have been a Melanie? That wasn't my fault — that I met her before you came along.'

'No, I know that. But it doesn't alter things now, does it? Please, let's be sensible and adult about this. Leave me alone.'

There was another pause. Sue turned her face away from the 'phone so that he should not hear her uneven quickened breathing. She wasn't sure if she could keep this up much longer. She was near to tears.

'Look, Sue — you've left all your winter clothes here. You'll need them sooner or later. You'll have to come over and collect them so why not come now? I've taken the day off. I'm at the flat. We could meet, as you say, like two sensible adults, talk things over and then, if you still feel you want to go, I'll fade out of the picture. That's fair enough, isn't it? There's no earthly reason why we shouldn't lunch together, anyhow.'

'No!' Sue cried sharply. A strange wave of gratitude to Ross suddenly swept over her. 'I can't. I've got a date.'

'Don't make idle excuses, darling!'

'I have. I have!' she repeated.

'With that man? What the hell is his name?'

'I can't see that it matters to you, but since you ask it's Ross Bryant.'

'Not that chap who's the chairman of Bryant & Coles steel works? I've met him.

Good God, Sue, the man's illiterate — self-made — impossible!'

The colour rose to Sue's cheeks.

'This is the nineteen-nineties. That's rubbish. He's an extremely nice, intelligent man.'

'And would my little Sue have made a friend of him if he hadn't been so well off?'

Now she was really angry — angry as only Paul could make her, jibing at her, sadistic, cruel and sneering.

'Once and for all, I'm not *your* Sue and I choose my own friends. I *like* Ross Bryant and I *don't* want to see you *ever* again. Is that clear?'

Disconcertingly, Paul suddenly laughed.

'Keep calm, my love, I'd almost forgotten what an intense little girl you are. So you can't lunch with me. Very well, then come after lunch. You might as well, Sue. We've got to get things cleared up. Lots of the stuff here is yours — apart from your clothes. If you aren't coming back to me, I shall probably give up the flat and I won't know what to do with your particular treasures. You know, darling, if you don't come, I shall always believe it's because you don't trust yourself to stand firm. Quite frankly, I don't think you really mean this break to be permanent — it's just your way of showing me that you can be independent if you want to be.'

'Paul, I'm NOT coming back!' she almost shouted in her effort to make him accept the truth.

'I'll believe that when you say it to my face!' was Paul's reply. 'Now I must go, darling. Without you here I have all the dreary shopping to do if I'm ever to have a meal at home. See you some time after your lunch with the wealthy tycoon. After all, you've nothing to be afraid of, have you, now you've stopped loving me?'

Damn him! Damn, *damn* him! Sue thought as she replaced the receiver. I won't see him. I won't ever go back to him. He's horrible. How could I ever have loved him? I hate, hate, *hate* him . . .

She began feverishly to clean the flat. She and Mary took turns with the shopping and cooking and had a daily in three mornings a week. Sue was not over-fond of polishing silver but now she went about the job, hoping to calm the storm of emotion that raged in her heart. She sat in the dining-room rubbing up Mary's silver as though it was of colossal importance that it should shine.

When she left the flat to meet Ross she was dressed with exaggerated care. She made herself as attractive as possible for Ross. She told herself that she owed him this as if in some way, her appearance could compensate for Paul's disparaging remarks. She wore a thin wool suit in pale, aquamarine blue with a paisley silk shirt of the same colour. She left her fair hair uncovered, very conscious of the fact that Ross admired it. He'd said so in France.

She did not notice the many male glances turned in her direction when she was in the Underground. She was wrapped up in her thoughts.

Ross was instantly appreciative as she walked into the hotel where he had been anxiously waiting for her.

'You're very punctual, Sue. You look lovely. Every time I see you, I think you are even more beautiful than before.'

'Why, thank you!' she said, imitating the American woman's manner of receiving a compliment. Remembering the shared joke, they both laughed and Sue began to relax. It was good to be with Ross again.

'You're so nice, Ross. You always make me laugh.'

'Except for last night!'

She shot him a quick look and saw that he had meant no more nor less than the words he spoke.

'Let's have a drink, shall we?'

He led her to the American bar. They

found a quiet table. He ordered Martinis and sat back in his chair.

'Feeling better this morning?' he asked gently. 'You certainly look it!'

She decided suddenly to be completely honest with Ross. He was far too nice for a woman to cheat and besides she had no wish to deceive him.

'I've spoken to Paul. He saw me at the restaurant last night and rang up this morning. I wouldn't have answered the 'phone but Mary was out and I thought it might be you again, Ross. Paul rang just after I'd talked to you.'

She noticed with surprise that his hands were a little unsteady — the only sign he gave that her news about Paul disturbed him.

'And?' he prompted quietly.

She tried to make her voice flippant.

'He tried to persuade me to go back to him. I refused. He wanted me to lunch with him today, but, thanks to you, I was able to say I was already committed.'

Ross's face cleared. He smiled.

'Then I've been of some use,' he said. 'Now perhaps I can persuade you to dine with me as well?'

She was saved a reply by the waiter arriving with their drinks. Ross paid him, leaving, as usual, an over-generous tip on the tray. In order to divert him, she said:

'You really are generous. Joe would have a fit if he saw you give so much to the waiters.'

Ross raised his eyebrows.

'I don't do it for effect, you know,' he said calmly. 'Your brother-in-law might imagine I am trying to create an impression. I'm not. I can't forget, you see, that there was a time when I was a damn sight worse off than that waiter. I can afford to give some of my cash away and I enjoy it. I believe if you make money, you should spend it. Not all, obviously. Perhaps what I'm really trying to say is that I intend to enjoy what I've made. No putting aside for a rainy day. Maybe if I was married and had children I'd be more careful. I don't know.'

'You should have children!' she said warmly. 'You'd make a wonderful father, Ross.'

He looked pleased.

'You really think so? I'd like kids — I'd like to have had *your* children, Sue. Does that sound over-the-top?'

She shook her head, silenced. She, too, would have liked a family. It was one of the reasons she'd wanted marriage with Paul and not a relationship in which successful contraception became of paramount importance; a top priority. Once she had believed she didn't care if she had a child of Paul's, without marriage; but Paul was never incautious; never allowed a mistake. She knew he was right but it had been another drop in the bucket of her bitterness.

'Sue, I've lost you again. If you must think about Paul when you are with me, I'd really prefer you talked out loud. At least we could discuss the man together and I'd try to help.'

She flushed, embarrassed, knowing she could not have told Ross these secret thoughts.

'Don't you feel free to tell me everything? Anything?' he asked quite sadly. 'The fact that I'm in love with you should make it possible, not make you draw right away, frightened of me, of what I'd think!'

'Oh, Ross!' She was conscious of such a mixture of feelings; sadness, bitterness, objection, doubt. A hopeless mixture, she thought. 'I hope you don't really mean that — about being in love with me,' she said suddenly. 'I'm a dead loss and the sooner you wake up to that fact, the better. I couldn't marry you, Ross. I'm not in love with you. I never will be.'

'Because of the kind of man I am? Or because of Paul?'

'Partly because of the kind of man you are — but I'm *not* referring to your background which I think is what you meant. I don't care a damn about that, Ross, I really don't. You are so nice; too kind, too generous. I would never have anything to give you in return. And that's where Paul comes in. I'm still in love with him. I know it's crazy. I know nothing good can come of it, but it doesn't stop the way I feel. I still love him, Ross, still belong to him.'

Ross stared at her, his eyes narrowed.

'*Why?*'

The single word startled her. She sighed.

'I don't know. I just know I belong to Paul. He wants me back and I want to go to him. I'm not even very happy with him but I'm a hundred times more unhappy away from him. Doesn't make sense, does it? I know he isn't really much good — as a person. He's weak and not always truthful; he's sometimes cruel and always selfish. I know all that but it doesn't seem to make any difference.'

'I think you should marry me!'

She stared at him, wide-eyed, not sure if she could have heard him correctly. He said again slowly: '*Marry me, Sue*. I know you're in love with Paul. I know you don't love me, but I think I could make you happy. I suppose that sounds terribly conceited, especially coming from someone like me, to a girl like you. But you see, I love you and I think you need me. Marry me, darling. Let me look after you. Let me love you the way you should be loved. Let me give you the sort of home you'd like, children, beautiful things to wear, beautiful places to see. Let me try to make your life altogether beautiful — worth living.'

'Ross, don't!' The cry escaped Sue involuntarily. Couldn't he understand that his wonderful breath-taking proposal was positively dangerous — threatening to break down her resistance? Tempting her to take the easy way out of her problems? encouraging her to go against all her most important standards and just accept all he offered. God knows he offered plenty. It would be so easy to say 'yes' — to put the hopeless difficulties connected with Paul into the past. To bury them so deep they could never be extricated again. For if ever she *did* marry Ross, she would be faithful to him and she'd never see Paul again.

'I can't, I can't!' she whispered. 'I might want to, but I can't. It would be wrong, unfair to you. I know it would. Please, Ross, don't ask me again — or at least, not until I am free of Paul and I'm not yet.'

Her words meant more to Ross than she could have imagined. He had not for one moment expected that she might seriously

132

consider his proposal. That she had done so, even vaguely admitting that she was tempted to say 'yes', was beyond his wildest hopes. He fully understood why she refused him now. Sue was honest to a degree which often hurt and this was another example of her honesty. She was virtually saying: *I can't start to love you because I still love Paul.* Well, that was all right by Ross. He knew that much already. He had only hoped he could help her to get over her disastrous love-affair.

She *had* been happy in France. Ross knew it intuitively. She had almost forgotten Paul Manton when she was with him; forgotten him sufficiently to spend that last night with him, Ross, in La Napoule. She had admitted that much before they fell asleep. In the bar at the Dorchester today, Ross had seen her — lovely, passionate, fulfilled, as she had murmured: 'You make me forget him, Ross . . .'

He could do it again. He could think up a thousand ways to put that other man out of her mind, her life, her thoughts. If only she would trust him, give him the chance.

'Lunch!' he said with one of his sudden changes of conversation that startled and sometimes amused her. 'Let's order a wonderful meal, Sue, and this time no leaving it half eaten. Okay?'

'Okay!' she agreed and once more, she was smiling.

Ross's ability to drag her out of herself was one of the qualities she most valued in him; and the way he spoiled her. He gave of himself so generously and naturally and with amazing sensibility and understanding. She was quite convinced that he was not deliberately laying a trap for her; that he never put on a show just to attract and impress her in order to gain his own ends. She was sure Ross was incapable of such conduct or in fact, of deliberate deceit.

She thought of Mary's scornful rejection of the man because of his background. It showed how little her sister knew about men like Ross; showed how little she herself had known of the way 'the other half' behaved before she'd met and grown to respect Ross Bryant.

She was suddenly glad and proud to be with him. He stood out in the room full of men, many distinguished, none better looking. Ross glowed with health and strength.

When lunch was finished, Ross once more brought up the question of the secretarial post at his office. But once again Sue found herself procrastinating. To accept the job meant to accept Ross as a part of her daily life and this was, in a way, committing herself to him. If by some remote chance, she ever did go back to live with Paul, it would be putting Ross as well as herself in a very awkward position. He might then not even wish to continue their friendship. How could he? If he loved her, how could he accept her going back to Paul?

Suddenly Sue knew what she must do. She must stop letting circumstances and other people direct her life. She must take the reins into her own hands; stop being afraid to face Paul again; stop being afraid of her own weak will. She must face him, tell him once and for all that she would never go back to him. Then, and only then, could she reach a decision about working for and with Ross.

'I'll tell you tomorrow,' she said. 'Will you give me another twenty-four hours to think it over?'

He agreed but he felt curiously depressed. He could not see that another day would solve anything. At the same time, their friendship was still so new, despite the extraordinary fact that they had been lovers! He must not rush things when Sue was in her present frame of mind. He was a man to make swift decisions, which, once taken, he carried out whole-heartedly. This strength of will and character were what had got him to his present position of affluence and he could not have changed himself even if he had desired to do so. At the same time, he understood Sue's hesitation. The only major decision she had made in her adult life had turned out to be completely disastrous. It was understandable that she should want to be very sure not to do the wrong thing again.

Quietly he pointed out to her that the job in his London office was quite apart from the one he had offered her earlier as his wife. He felt, he said, that she would enjoy the work as a P.A. — a personal assistant to him would be different from the job held by one who had to spend her days merely taking and transcribing shorthand. Sue would arrange business luncheons; help to organise board meetings, and supervise the conference room; deal with his private appointments, arrange air flights or train schedules when he had to travel on business, perhaps on occasions even accompany him.

'Don't you have anyone to do all this for you now?' Sue asked curiously.

Ross grinned.

'Yes, but she's pretty long in the tooth and due for retirement. You wouldn't be doing my Miss Goodman out of a job. In fact she has already asked me to replace her. Quite frankly, I've not so far found anyone suitable, anyone I can trust and get on with. You'll probably laugh at this, but I need someone with your background. Old Miss Goodman's an admiral's daughter and many is the time I've blessed the occasions when she's put me right in social matters. You probably take such things for granted, Sue, but I've had to learn the right way to do things. I owe Miss Goodman quite a lot — she's been with me since the days when I first started to make a go of things. I'd like to retire her with a good pension. All I need is someone to replace her.'

Sue felt a renewed interest in the job. She would enjoy the kind of work Ross described and she liked the idea of being necessary in all kinds of ways.

But after she had said goodbye to him and sat in the taxi he had insisted upon paying in advance, she felt his influence fade. As she drove through Hyde Park towards Marble Arch, she found herself tapping on the window and telling the driver to drop her off at Selfridges. She was not yet ready to go back to the Hampstead flat and Mary's anxious questioning.

She bought nothing in the store. Going in to the cafeteria for a cup of tea at half past four, she finally admitted to herself that she had not really intended to buy anything. She had just wanted a way to fill in the afternoon — fill in time.

She drank her tea slowly. Five minutes later she was in a bus on her way to Paul's flat.

8

Paul sat looking at Sue, his grey eyes excited but narrowed thoughtfully. He had not made the mistake of trying to take her in his arms when she first walked into the room.

'You're looking marvellous, Sue,' he had said. 'Obviously the South of France suited you.'

She tried to keep her eyes away from the graceful, slender figure stretched out in the armchair. She felt self-conscious and wretchedly nervous and stood with her back to the fireplace, looking down at him.

He seemed different in some strange, indefinable way; not a stranger yet not the same Paul. She wondered if he had changed; suffered a little because she had left him, and if he really had been lonely and miserable; or if it was just the contrast between Paul and Ross whose large square frame and obvious masculinity had become more familiar to her than Paul's lithe grace.

It was not that he was effeminate but he was less overwhelmingly male than Ross. Paul Manton was of medium height, slenderly built with rather large, expressive grey eyes

139

which could at times look remarkably cold. He had smooth, fair brown hair which he wore long and was brushed back over both ears. She often used to tell him that the day would come when he had 'silver wings' and would look most distinguished. His mouth was beautifully shaped.

He had taken off his tailored grey jacket and was sprawled in the armchair, a leg over one side; his white shirt was, as always, spotless; his tie quiet, expensive.

Nothing has changed here, she thought poignantly, except that it was all rather untidy and not very well cleaned. It lacked the woman's touch. The big attractively shaped sitting room overlooking the King's Road was full of sunshine today. She and Paul had always loved the sun. It showed up the beautiful paintings they had chosen together over the years. One, a scene of Marseilles in a gilt frame hanging over the fireplace, was after the style of Monet. Paul knew a lot about art. He had bought this in Paris, a present for what he called their 'first anniversary'. A wonderful if rather surrealistic oil of a nude woman hung at the other end of the room. That was an original and worth quite a lot of money. Both these belonged to Paul. He had taught her about painting just as he had taught her about sex, and in doing so, had turned her from the rather unsophisticated girl she had been into a woman of experience.

They had decided upon the décor together although she accepted the fact that Paul's taste predominated. He did have good taste. Now, looking around, she saw anew the yellow silk curtains with the pale blue carpet and the yellow brocade sofa and chairs she had helped Paul choose, the striking looking blue velvet Queen Anne winged chair, and the Louis Quinze writing bureau.

The door to the bedroom was shut but she knew only too well what lay behind it: one huge, low double bed with a grey covered headboard and matching bedspread, a grey carpet. They had both been pleased with the shock of the brilliant pink and silver curtains and the silver painted dressing table that ran the length of the wall, with the long mirror above it. Paul had given it to her one Christmas.

There were the same books in the flat but no flowers. She remembered with a stab of pain that it was she who usually bought the flowers. Towards the end, she had bought her own presents, too. He would throw her a fifty pound note and say carelessly:

'I'm so busy, sweet. You choose what you want, will you?'

'Well, Paul,' she said, trying to speak with indifference, 'I've come as you suggested to pack up my clothes and possessions. I think I should get down to it, don't you?'

He ignored her remark.

'I'm glad you came, Sue. You can see what kind of a mess the flat's got into without you. I positively loathe the place on my own.' He paused, watching her face intently. 'I've missed you desperately.'

He saw the colour rush into her cheeks and her hands clutch at her bag nervously. He knew her so well, he could exactly judge her mood. She was afraid of this — of the power he had always had over her.

'I came as you suggested, to collect my belongings, Paul,' she repeated.

'Did you?'

He stood up now. He was only a little taller than Sue but she at once felt overwhelmed by him. She moved backwards until she was actually leaning against the mantel shelf.

'Let's have a drink!' Paul went on as though he had not noticed her withdrawal. He walked over to the cocktail cabinet where the drinks were kept. 'The usual?' he asked, turning his face to her again. She nodded, her throat dry, her brow suddenly damp.

Paul was so much in command of himself, so entirely self-possessed! Sue remembered with a sharp clarity that he never lost his temper; never to her knowledge lost complete control; no, not even when they were at the very zenith of love-making. She, in contrast, could lose her grip on sense and reality so easily. In an argument, she would sooner or later end in tears; in a quarrel, her surrender would be as complete and utter as her original anger, because she could not bear to be angry with him or feel his displeasure. Once he had refused to speak to her for two days and she had been so much at her wit's end that she had beseeched him to talk to her, even apologising for what she had very well known had been his mistake — not hers. And when they made love . . .

'Well, here's to us, darling!'

She shivered and clinked her glass against his. Over the rim, their gaze met. Paul's did not waver like hers.

'You're coming back, of course!' he said quietly.

'No, I'm *not*! I don't want to. You don't seem to realise it, but I was very unhappy with you.'

'But, darling, of *course* I realise it. It was a good thing you did leave me — it's done me good and made me see things from your point of view instead of only from my own. I've been much too egotistical. I don't ever want to go back to the *old* way of life.'

He saw her startled expression, followed by a look almost of panic. He went on:

'You must see things from my point of view, too. I wanted to get married just as much as you did, Sue, only I dreaded the thought of upsetting Melanie and the child. No one likes hurting people — especially children. The kid is fond of me. Not unnatural! Melanie and I seemed to have settled down reasonably happily — it was only occasionally we had those scenes and you'd bring up the subject of divorce. I suppose I should have realised that marriage meant much more to you than you let on. Nothing mattered much to me so long as we were together, Sue, but I see now that this was an entirely selfish point of view. Well, that's all changed. I'm not living with Melanie any more.'

Sue's eyes grew enormous with incredulity.

'You mean you've actually *left* her?'

Paul poured himself another drink, his face hidden from Sue.

'Not exactly *physically* departed the house. But it isn't married life any longer. We lead our own separate lives. For all I know, Melanie's got a boyfriend. She would probably welcome a divorce herself now if I asked her for one.'

Sue finished her own drink quickly. She tried to sort out her confused thoughts. So Paul was on the brink of a divorce. Things had changed with a vengeance! She wouldn't, if she wanted to return to Paul, need to feel any moral responsibility for the break up of a marriage that had already ended. Paul and Melanie were leading separate lives. The divorce was now only a question of technicalities.

'So you see, my darling, I need you quite desperately.' She heard Paul's charming voice. 'I've nothing to live for except you. I need you more than I ever did.'

He put down his drink and came across the room. He took the empty glass from Sue's hand and slowly, tenderly, he drew her into his arms. For a single instant of time, Sue stood stiff and irresolute in his embrace. Then she let out her breath in one glad cry:

'*Paul!*'

She hugged him, both arms around his neck. She felt as if she had come home. This was where she belonged; always had belonged — in Paul's arms. No one else in the world mattered. She could never be happy apart from him, for she *was* part of him; her whole body merged into his with a remembered familiarity that was gloriously comforting and seemed so absolutely right.

His mouth hardened against hers. He began to caress her with a quick delicate touch, knowing her body, rediscovering it, drawing the familiar response. Everything he did to her was new and yet not new, for they were only going back to the past shared passion. It was, too, as though their recent separation lent a special enchantment to every touch, every kiss, and sharpened their sensibilities.

Feverishly they kissed and caressed each other.

As had happened many times before, Paul would not wait to take her through to the bedroom in order to enjoy the freedom of the wide double bed. He undressed her with practised ease and laid her on the sofa.

'If I were a painter, I would adore to paint you just like this,' he whispered, his eyes hot with desire as he stared hungrily at the golden brown body against the yellow of the sofa cushions. He traced the white lines where the sun had not touched her small breasts, her slender girl's hips.

'Here and here and here, no one but I have seen or kissed you, my love.'

Quickly, Sue drew his head down to hers, unwilling for him to see the expression in her eyes. She felt more guilty than any adulterous wife. She could never tell Paul about Ross, never explain it. At this moment, she could not understand it herself.

It was not in Paul's nature to lose himself completely in the act of love. His enjoyment was slow, sensuous, partly derived from his power to evoke total surrender in the woman he held rather than his own enjoyment of the act. Not even his increased desire for Sue could destroy his extraordinary command of himself. He did not wish to surrender to Sue completely. To him this would represent weakness. He wanted complete control of her. He had seen too many men become slaves to their women; ending as they always did, by being dependent upon them, dominated by them. His own mother had dominated and influenced his father, leaving him emasculated, a pathetic thing in Paul's sight, without the courage to stand up to his wife. Paul had not been very old when he first realised that an appeal to his father was a waste of breath if he wanted to counteract his mother's wishes.

Through the years of his adolescence, Paul learned how best to achieve his own ends with his mother. Her adoration of her clever, charming, attractive son made everything easy once he knew how to use her love as a weapon. When he wished to be a match for her, he found the way was to withdraw his own affection. This could immediately weaken her. By the time he was of age, he could do anything he wanted simply by refusing to admit that he cared if she tried to argue with him.

He had not found this dictum for living quite so simple with the other women in his life. He had no real love for his mother and little need of her once he'd left school. But with the girls he desired, he had wanted something from them. He made the mistake of letting Melanie discover his own power. Until the advent of Sue, his young wife had often bested him in marital arguments by refusing him admission to her bed. She had used sex as a trump card and for a while, he had known himself the weaker of the two. But once he met and fell for Sue, his physical need of Melanie ceased to have such importance and finally died altogether. So slowly, his wife was forced to realise that her trump card held no value after all.

In many ways Melanie continued to hold his respect. She had not accepted the new situation without looking for and finding alternative means of getting her own way. She used the child, to whom she knew Paul was very attached; but mostly she used money. Unlike Paul, who was dependent upon his own earnings, Melanie had private capital and income. Paul could support them on his salary but the luxuries they both enjoyed came out of Melanie's money — the Mercedes he ran, the M.G. she personally used; the nanny, the heated swimming pool; the holidays abroad, the weekend parties when Paul could entertain his associates lavishly enough to earn him quick promotion if it was in the offing.

If Melanie knew about Sue, she kept quiet about it; just as Paul kept quiet about Melanie's affairs. Very occasionally, when presumably Melanie was without a lover, she would indicate to Paul that he was welcome to return to the marital bed. He never refused such offers, knowing from one bitter experience that Melanie would pay him back for the insult in some seemingly unconnected manner — the cancellation of a dinner party which was important to him, or a threat that she couldn't possibly afford this or that with her housekeeping allowance.

She was tiny in stature — a petite dark girl with a fringe and a small delicate heart-shaped face, who could look fourteen when she chose. She was now in her thirties. In character she was as tough as himself. When he first met Sue, it was her gentleness, her dependence, her vulnerability that had drawn him to her; that and her innocence. Melanie, he had discovered, had certainly not been as innocent or ignorant, as she had led him to believe. But there was no doubting Sue's ignorance. Her boarding school seemed to be run on almost Victorian lines and her home life in the holidays had been as restricted, with that old brigadier father of hers practically standing guard over his two pretty daughters with his shotgun.

Paul used to laugh at the brigadier at one time — though he'd certainly never laughed in his face. But a little later, when he'd finally talked Sue into moving into his flat permanently, he'd been a little apprehensive of the old chap. He *could* harm Paul at the Foreign Office. He had influential friends there. Paul had held his breath uneasily, banking on the fact that Sue's father would take no action that would harm his little fledgling. If Paul's reputation was besmirched, then Sue's would suffer more.

The gamble paid off. The brigadier cut Sue off without the proverbial penny but neither he, Paul, nor Sue had cared. They were both too happily enthralled in their love-making.

Yes, he had loved and did still love Sue in his curious egotistical way. She had over the years become necessary to him. Not only did her utter devotion flatter and compliment him, but she managed successfully to anticipate his every whim, to spoil him in a way Melanie never had done and never would do. Melanie would consider such behaviour debasing. She liked her men at her feet and certainly never, or as far as he knew, had she laid her heart at theirs.

He'd wondered sometimes about his wife's boyfriends. One or two he knew, for a certainty. But just how many there were and how often Melanie saw them, she kept skilfully concealed from her husband. There had developed a tacit understanding between them that neither should probe too deep below the surface of an outwardly successful marriage. The present situation suited them both. It was only Sue's endless persistence that she wanted marriage that spoiled Paul's peace.

He felt a moment of unusual tenderness for her today, as she lay quiet now in his arms, an enchantingly happy smile on her face. Dear little Sue. She was so ingenuous. It was so easy, really, to make her happy. She was such pure delight to love. In many ways, she was more beautiful and desirable now than she had been when he had first seduced her. The rounded teenager had matured into a graceful slender woman. Only her face was a little too bony, perhaps, the cheekbones high, prominent beneath the shadowed blue eyes. He touched one cheek with his fingertip and she caught his hand and pressed her lips against it.

'I love you, Paul. I always have. I always will.'

He kissed her gently, responsive as always to her flattery and pleased by his mastery over her. He loved her most at times like this when he knew he could ask anything of her and that she would comply.

'I love you, too, my darling!' he whispered back. 'We're going to be so happy together again — happier than we ever were. Never, never leave me again, Sue. I couldn't bear it.'

'Neither could I!' she said huskily.

She linked her hands behind his head and looked trustingly into his grey eyes. Now, here like this, it was impossible to believe that she had had the strength or the desire to leave him. He was her man, her life. It had always astounded her that Paul could love *her* . . . she seemed to have so little to offer him. She'd never been particularly clever — Mary was the brainy one — and Paul was brilliant. He had advanced astonishingly quickly at the Foreign Office. Even Mary, the critic, had admitted that he was highly intelligent.

Sue had heard it said that opposites often attracted each other, but still she could not understand how Paul could need her so desperately. She was too lacking in vanity to admit that she was more beautiful or intelligent than any other girl he had known.

Suddenly, she thought of Ross who had found her not only beautiful but utterly irresistible and infinitely superior.

'*Poor Ross!*'

She had not known she had spoken the words aloud but Paul, leaning on one elbow, stared down at her sharply.

'Ross? The man I saw you with at the restaurant? Tell me about him. Is he in love with you? Does he want to marry you? You aren't in love with him, are you?'

Sue hid her face against his neck.

'Of course not,' she said. 'But I like him and I dislike the idea of hurting him. He asked me to accept a job as his secretary — as a sort of P.A. I had promised to consider it, but I suppose I'll have to turn the job down now. He'll be very disappointed.'

Paul relaxed, gently stroking a damp tendril of hair from her forehead.

'Of course you'll have to turn it down,' he said in a slow drawling voice. 'Quite definitely. I want you here with me.'

9

Melanie sat at her dressing table, her back to Paul as meticulously she painted her nails. Every now and again she glanced into her mirror, her dark slanting eyes narrowed thoughtfully as she observed her husband's profile. The coolness of her voice gave no hint of the tumult of feeling that burned inside her.

Of all the things he had said and done in the last half hour to annoy her, his total disregard for her as a woman angered her most. Any other man, she thought bitterly, would have been well aware of her desirability at this moment. The black, lace-topped camisole was as provocative as the carefully exposed white thighs — one crossed delicately over the other. The new black lace stockings accentuated their slimness of line. She wore no bra. Her small pointed breasts needed no artificial support and she knew that this was usually a sure way of exciting Paul.

He lounged at the foot of her bed, fully dressed, chain smoking, his conversation edgy and disjointed as if he could not bring himself to confess to the real reason for his presence in her bedroom at this time when he should be dressing for dinner. Yet she saw that he had not once looked in her direction.

With a cat-like instinct, Melanie had guessed that he had something important on his mind which he was finding difficult to express. All her senses warned her it would not be a pleasant revelation but her nature was such that she preferred to know exactly what she was up against before she had to do battle with Paul on any issue.

Their marriage, she thought, had for long been more of an armed neutrality than a union, yet there had been a time when Paul was crazily in love with her; unable to leave her alone. His desire used to be quite insatiable. He had been easy to manage then. Now it was different. Paul had found himself another woman and regained his independence. At the time, it suited her for she was having a heady affair with one of their married friends. Now she realised that she'd been a fool to let Paul slip from her grasp. He was still attractive to her when she had no love affair on the boil and his total lack of sexual interest in her now was a deliberate insult. She wanted all men to desire her.

'Isn't it time you got changed, Paul?' she asked for the second time. 'You don't want to keep Sir Henry waiting, I'm sure!'

Tonight's dinner party was mostly for Paul's benefit. Sir Henry Bagland was a fairly new acquaintance and a man with considerable political influence who might well be useful to Paul in his job. Normally Paul was as ruthlessly ambitious as Melanie herself, and let nothing stand in the way of such an occasion as this. But tonight he was acting as though Sir Henry was of little or no importance. Melanie was baffled.

'I suppose I should get a move on,' Paul's voice was slow, perfectly modulated, but still he made no move.

'Anything you particularly want to discuss?' she asked, studying her nails.

Paul drew in his breath. Melanie was sharp — she'd guessed he had something important to say. There was something positively feline about his beautiful wife; ruthless; cunning; insidious.

'As a matter of fact there is. I want you to give me a divorce!'

The little bottle of nail varnish tipped over on the glass top of the dressing table. Melanie swore and began to mop up the sticky mess with a face tissue. The smell of acetone filled the room. The spilt bottle was the only outward sign Melanie gave of the shock Paul's request had given her.

'Don't be a fool!' she said sharply. She decided to try ridicule. 'If that's all you have to say, then please hurry up and go and change. I'm not in the mood for a joke at the moment.'

Paul's mouth tightened.

'It's no joke. I'm serious, Melanie. I want a divorce.'

Melanie kept her head averted. She lent over casually and patted a straying hair into place.

'Then you'll just have to want,' she said harshly. 'End of discussion. Get changed, please.'

Paul swung his legs off the bed and stood up, his face white and angry.

'You're not going to ignore this, Melanie. I tell you I'm serious. I really mean it this time.'

Melanie gave an artificial laugh.

'You *really* meant it last time!' she said with sarcasm. 'For goodness sake grow up, Paul. You're old enough to have affairs without complicating the issue with a load of romantic nonsense.'

'I'm not being romantic, my dear — merely practical. The girl in question insists on the proprieties — a certificate of marriage.'

To his acute irritation, Melanie gave a shout of genuine laughter.

'My poor darling!' she said, pushing out

her lower lip. 'And you really believe I'm going to give you my blessing just like that?'

Paul took a step towards her.

'Why not? You aren't in love with me. You don't really care if I'm here or not. We lead separate lives anyway, don't we?'

Melanie looked up at him from beneath long dark lashes.

'But, Paul, whether I love you or not doesn't alter the fact that I still find you attractive. In fact, when you're angry with me as you are now, you raise all my baser passions, my pet. If it wasn't for Sir Henry, I'd go to bed with you right now.'

'You disgust me!' Paul said brutally. But the worst of it was, he had suddenly discovered that he wanted Melanie, just as she wanted him. Love didn't come into it. If they were in bed together, they would become two selfish demanding animals.

He turned quickly from the sight of her small white breasts clearly revealed beneath the black lace. He tried to think of Sue but could remember only the feel of Melanie's sensuous body when she was as avid for sex as himself and could meet him on exactly the same terms. There was something almost masculine in her basic approach to sex but she herself was totally and completely female — as female as a Siamese cat.

158

She grimaced at him in the mirror.

'Oh, do go and change, Paul!' her cool voice taunted him. 'If you must persist with this nonsense, let's carry on later after Sir Henry has gone.'

Paul left her bedroom without speaking. He knew that by leaving he had allowed her to win the first round but he did not dare stay whilst his body was so uncomfortably conscious of hers. Melanie would know it with the strange perception of hers and the very last thing he wanted was to end up in bed with her. In bed she always emerged the victor.

The formal dinner party wound its slow, boring way through the evening. Melanie had, as usual, done everything to perfection. The pre-dinner drinks were exactly right; iced, delicious. The dinner table glistened with Georgian silver, Waterford glass and shimmering candlelight. She, herself, tiny and vivacious in black chiffon, was flirting with old Sir Henry using every bit of charm she could muster. The meal was well cooked — Melanie had an excellent cordon bleu girl. Over brandy and cigars, Sir Henry mellowed.

'Congratulate you, m'boy — delightful little wife — perfect hostess. Go far with you, that charming creature.'

Paul was torn between satisfaction at the

effect Melanie had on Sir Henry and irritation because the silly old fool had fallen so easily to the bait. He was irritated, too, because Sir Henry was absolutely right — Melanie was the perfect hostess; the perfect wife for an up-and-coming diplomat, attractive with her almond eyes and dark satin hair, charming, intelligent, clever and socially right. By comparison, Sue would seem a child, ingenuous — even shy — but then, of course, she was years younger than Melanie. He sometimes forgot Sue was only twenty-four and Melanie, like himself, in the thirties.

His earlier annoyance with his wife began to veer towards Sue. It was quite obvious she had no idea how her insistence on a divorce and re-marriage was going to complicate his life. Nearly all his friends — the ones who mattered to his career — liked and admired Melanie. They'd think him a fool to leave her for a young, inexperienced girl. Not that Sue was unattractive — very far from it. She was lovely and she might well strike many of his friends as a good deal more attractive than Melanie. But she lacked Melanie's drive and social *savoir faire*; she lacked the ruthless ambition with which Melanie strove to forward his career, wanting his success every bit as much as he did.

During coffee he listened to his wife

160

commiserating with Sir Henry about the recent loss of his wife. She sounded utterly sincere in her sympathies, and yet an hour before Paul had heard her say:

'Thank God that dreary old bag of a wife kicked the bucket. At least we won't have to endure *her* this evening!'

Despite himself, Paul grinned. It amused him to see the powerful Sir Henry lapping up Melanie's insincerities.

'Must see what we can do for you, m'boy!' Sir Henry said when he was about to leave later that night. 'Your wife tells me you haven't had any promotion for the past two years. Can't have our best young blood stagnating like this. Quite enough of a brain drain to the States as it is. I'll see Burgoyne tomorrow — find out if there isn't a higher place for a promising young man like you in the office, what?'

When the old boy had gone, Melanie raised her glass of brandy and touched Paul's glass. She was looking flushed and pleased with herself.

'Here's to your speedy promotion,' she said. 'Think he really will see Lord Burgoyne tomorrow?'

Paul shrugged. He was fairly hopeful and he knew if anything came of this, it was entirely due to Melanie's efforts.

'Thanks!' he said grudgingly. 'It went off very well!'

Melanie sank down on the soft white-tweed covered sofa, kicking off her stiletto heeled shoes and tucking her legs beneath her. She yawned.

'Thank God, it's Sunday tomorrow — we can stay in bed all morning and read the papers.'

Paul's hands tightened round his glass. He'd promised Sue he would go back to the flat tomorrow. If he didn't she'd be upset.

'I might have to go back to Town,' he said hesitantly. 'Got a bit of work to catch up on . . . '

He broke off, uncomfortably aware of Melanie's raised eyebrows and amused eyes.

'You mean you want to report back to the girl friend that I refused to divorce you.'

Paul lit a cigarette with unsteady fingers. No one could annoy him more quickly than Melanie when she spoke in that cool, derisive voice. He scowled at her but she yawned again carelessly.

'Do have a grain of sense, Paul. You'd gain nothing and lose everything if I did agree to a divorce. How do you imagine old gaffers like Sir Henry would view such proceedings? Burgoyne's a Catholic. He'd side with me and you know it. Bang goes your promotion.'

162

'Maybe I don't care so much about my promotion,' Paul said sullenly. 'Maybe there are other things more important — like spending your life with someone who really does love you.'

'Oooh, I see!' Melanie drawled. 'This is Serious with a capital S. This is Romance with a capital R. Do tell me, Paul, is she someone new, or the same old flame?'

'I've never loved anyone but Sue!' Paul said, off guard. 'And what's more, she cares a hell of a lot more for me than you ever did!' he added defiantly. 'I don't expect you to understand what I'm talking about. I don't think you ever loved anyone but yourself. Well, I don't want to go on with a marriage that's empty of any real affection. I really do love Sue and I want to marry her.'

'And your son? Don't you care about *him?*' Paul flushed.

'Of course, but I'm willing to give him up to you. You can keep him, Melanie. I don't want to see him torn between us.'

'Very considerate!' Her voice was hard now. 'And what about me! Maybe I don't fancy the world knowing my husband has left me for another woman.'

'You'd soon marry again — you've plenty of admirers!' Now it was Paul's turn to be scornful. 'You're always ramming it down my throat how much you contribute to our marriage. Well, some man somewhere must be wanting all those many virtues you possess — not to mention your bank balance! And certainly not forgetting that beautiful body you like to offer as a good conduct prize.'

Melanie suddenly swung her legs onto the floor and stood up, her face white and furious.

'So that's my thanks for tonight and all the other times I've worked to back you up. Well, I'll tell you something, Paul. You may be fed up with me but I'm a damn sight more fed up with *you*. Go to that girl if you want to. Do you think I really mind? I fell out of love with you a long while ago. You bore me, do you understand? Bore me to tears. I used to think you were intelligent. Now I know you're a bloody fool. You never did know how to manage me and now you're going to make a mess of your career as well. Don't come running to me when you've got over your stupid little romance. If I divorce you, it'll be final. Think about it, Paul, *dear*. You might not find yourself such a howling success at the F.O. without little Melanie behind you. But that won't worry me. As you said so sweetly just now, I've plenty of other fish to fry.'

She flounced out of the room, head held

high, eyes flashing and slammed the door
violently behind her. Paul sat down in the
nearest chair. To his intense annoyance, his
legs and hands were trembling. The truth
about rows with Melanie was that there was
always an edge of truth in the spiteful things
she said to him. He *would* find it tough
without her to back him — particularly where
money was concerned. If she really did mean
to divorce him, she could raise a big enough
stink to damage him at the F.O., too. She had
a greater number of influential friends than
he had, in fact.

He tried to think of Sue and the intensity
of her love for him. Certainly as a woman, she
was worth ten of Melanie. She was everything
a man wanted at the end of a tiring day. She
never criticised, seldom argued. They never
disagreed except over the question of divorce.
Once they were married, there would be
complete peace. Melanie's violent outbursts,
restless nature, made any kind of peace
impossible under her roof. A man needed
peace — just as he needed love and the kind
of affection Sue lavished on him.

A little of his anger evaporated as he
imagined Sue's face when he told her
tomorrow that Melanie had finally agreed to
a divorce. She would radiate happiness and
gratitude; make him feel marvellous instead

of vaguely afraid. Her complete dependence upon him always increased his feelings of masculine superiority, invincibility. Melanie, on the other hand, undermined and demoralised him. Living with her was enough to make a man impotent. She was the kind of woman who could taunt a man into impotency, then taunt him again for being unable to satisfy her.

Paul relaxed, glanced at his watch and seeing that it was only a little after eleven, poured himself another brandy. He wondered what Sue was doing at this moment. She still hadn't moved back into the flat although she came there every evening. Poor little thing hadn't the courage to tell that bossy sister of hers she was going back to him. But she would, as soon as he could promise her the divorce she wanted so much. That would silence Mary.

This evening he knew Sue was dining out with that odd boyfriend she'd picked up in France. At first Paul hadn't wanted her to go. Then she had explained that it was only to tell the chap she couldn't take the job he'd offered her and that she wouldn't continue to see him. It hadn't been difficult to worm out of Sue the fact that this man was in love with her. Sue had also admitted that if the break between her and Paul himself had been final, she might have been weak enough to drift into marriage with the fellow.

'Not because I love him, Paul — I could never love anyone but you — but because he's always so kind.'

For the first time during his association with her, Paul had been jealous. He was glad she was giving Bryant the push. Couldn't be too soon for his liking. Pity about the job, though. Sue would have to work now. Without Melanie's money behind him, he would have a struggle to manage on his salary, especially if Melanie stung him for maintenance for the child as well as for herself. She didn't need it but she might well claim it nevertheless — out of spite. It would be like her.

Paul took another brandy. He felt a sudden chill. The thought of financial economies was depressing. He was only willing to face it because he was so much in love with Sue. Let Melanie deride love if she chose — she simply did not know what real love meant. But he did. He needed Sue far more than Melanie or the assets she brought to his life. For a long while, he had not realised just how much Sue did mean to him — he'd taken her pretty much for granted. It had been a hell of a shock the day she walked out on him. Now he was beginning to find her doubly desirable.

He thought eagerly of his reception tomorrow when he saw her and told her about the divorce.

10

'You look radiant, Sue — so well and so happy. It makes me happy just to look at you!'

Ross's voice was slightly husky with the emotion the sight of her roused in him. He no longer attempted to hide his love for her from himself or the rest of the world. He wanted to shout it aloud. Here, in the restaurant he would have liked to be able to stand up and say: 'This beautiful woman is mine — I love her more than anything in the world!'

Tonight, she seemed to him even more beautiful. There was a warm glow radiating from her and a smile which played tantalizingly at the corners of her mouth. He wanted terribly to kiss her; dared not remember that once he had held her all night long in his arms. Yet — remembering, he could not believe he had loved her as much then as he did now. This need of her and the intensity of his desire seemed to increase with every meeting.

He ordered drinks and sat for a moment quietly enjoying the thrill of being with her again.

'I wonder if you have any idea how much I love you!' he said at last.

The expression on her face changed. A slight shiver ran down Ross's spine.

'Ross, I have to talk to you. I thought we could have our meal first and I'd tell you afterwards but maybe that's wrong; maybe I should say at once what I must.'

She looked at his anxious face with a curious sense of despair. When she had agreed to meet him for dinner it had been because she knew she had to say goodbye to him; thank him for his friendship but tell him that it had to end because she was going back to Paul. Steeped in her happiness over Paul's promise to demand a divorce from Melanie this weekend, she had given no deep thought to Ross or what this decision would mean to him. Wrapped up in the cocoon of her own feelings, she had forgotten Ross's love for her. She felt suddenly ashamed, as though she had deliberately used him as a prop which she now intended to discard without a second thought because she had no further need of it.

'Oh, Ross!' she said wistfully, 'I feel so awful — so very sorry. I don't know how to say this so that you won't be hurt . . .'

'You're going back to him!' Ross's voice was ragged, torn, accusing.

170

The colour flooded her cheeks.

'Please, Ross, hear me out. I'm not going to be his mistress any more — he's going to marry me. This time he means to get a divorce. He really does love me, Ross. You have to believe that.'

The man beside her looked at her with eyes that were suddenly hard as well as bitter.

'You don't have to justify your decision to me, Sue. It isn't necessary I should understand. It isn't my business, really.'

Sue felt a lump gathering in her throat. Never had Ross spoken to her in that hard, cold voice — almost as though he despised her.

'But it is necessary!' she cried. 'You're my friend — the only friend I have. I couldn't bear it if I thought you had a poor opinion of me. Please try not to hate me, Ross!'

His face looked suddenly like that of a man in torment.

'How can I hate you, woman? I love you. I love you so much I can't stand the thought of you with another man. I'm jealous as hell. No doubt my social veneer is a very thin skin because, right now, I want nothing more than to beat the hell out of him. I don't hate you. I hate him!'

The violence in his voice frightened her. As

171

if aware of this, his face softened. He added gently.

'Sorry, Sue. It's been a shock — that's all. When you came out with me tonight, looking so well, so happy, I suppose I kidded myself it was because you were beginning to get over Paul at last; and that you were happy *with* *me*. It's all too easy, isn't it, when you want something desperately, to talk yourself into believing it is within your grasp. I should have known from the start you'd never be able to fall in love with someone like me. You're educated, intelligent. If you love this man, then there must be something special about him. I daresay in other circumstances I might like and enjoy his company. Oh, hell — Sue — please believe me, I wish you both every happiness,' he ended in a suffocated voice.

She sat silent, unable to cope with her own unexpected feeling of misery. Was it just a reflection of Ross's mood? She had not imagined this meeting with him would be so distressing. She ought to have foreseen it — to have written to him rather than told him face to face.

'I suppose this is the last time I'll see you, then?' Ross's voice was under control now. Only a trace of bitterness remained.

'I don't know. It depends. I'd like to keep you as a friend but ... '

'But a bit too much water has gone under the bridge!' Ross finished. 'I don't think I could be 'just friends' with you, Sue. I don't know if men and women who are at all attractive to each other can ever be successful as platonic friends. I certainly doubt if I could feel platonic about you. You're too attractive a woman for me to ignore that side of you. And maybe I'm too much of a man to become the nice calm faithful friend. No, I'd rather not see you again. At least, that's how I think I feel now. Maybe in time I might get used to the idea of you . . . and him. Not as things are.'

He turned and beckoned to the waiter, ordered two more Martinis without consulting her. She felt miserable — unable to think of anything to say that would help the situation. Suddenly, Ross covered her hand with his and held it in a fierce grip.

'You're the only woman I've wanted to marry!' he said. 'I know you're in love with Paul Manton; I'm glad for your sake that he's getting a divorce and will marry you, but I do want you to understand that although you don't love me and although you're in love with him, *I* still want you for my wife. Does that make any kind of sense? I want it so much, I don't think it is possible for me to see you occasionally as a casual friend. No matter how likable the man you intend to marry, I could never like him. He will have what I want and for that I can only hate him. Maybe my way of loving isn't as unselfish as it should be. I strongly suspect I'm one of these all-or-nothing men who can't accept half measures. Will you forgive me if I say I can't offer you just friendship?'

'Ross, you're making me feel awful. I'm the one who needs forgiveness. I've hurt you and there's nothing I meant to do less than that. I wish I had been free to love you. I envy the woman you will eventually marry. I mean that. Your way of loving is the way any woman wants to be loved. But you'll find someone else, Ross — someone who will make a much better wife than I ever could. Maybe when that happens, we will be able to be friends again. That would be so nice, wouldn't it? You'd bring your wife to dinner with Paul and me and we'd be able to laugh and tease each other about once having been 'old flames'. We could flirt a little and maybe steal a kiss or two under the mistletoe at Christmas, and your wife and my husband would be very jealous. I'd ask you to be godfather to my children and you'd make me godmother to one of yours . . . ' she broke off — her eyes stinging with sudden tears.

The waiter brought the drinks and Ross

released her hand in order to pay for them. When the waiter left them, he did not take possession of it again. He said quietly:

'What you've just said is quite improbable. I want you to be happy, Sue. Nothing else matters. Will you promise me one thing? If you find you *are* unhappy, you'll send for me? Forget what I've said to you about love and marriage. It isn't important. What is important is that you should know that I'll come to you, no matter where in the world I am, *if* you need me. Will you promise, Sue? Will you?'

'Ross, that wouldn't be fair. And I'm not going to be unhappy. Everything is all right now. I have great faith in Paul. He's changed completely — he's proved his love for me.'

'Yes, I know, but promise me all the same? Please?'

His voice was so serious, she could not refuse even while she did not fully understand why this promise should be so important to him. Once she gave it, he seemed to relax — to become once more the gentle, attentive companion she'd grown to know and in a strange way to need.

Their dinner was not the ordeal she had feared. Ross now talked of impersonal matters; particularly about a young red-headed 'Sloan' who had applied for the job as his P.A. Ross had told her to apply again in a few weeks' time, still hoping that Sue would agree to take the position. Now he thought he might well employ the girl, if she still seemed interested.

'She's only eighteen — very young but with all the trappings of sophistication,' Ross explained. 'I gathered at the interview that 'Mummy and Daddy' were dead set against her applying for the job. Mummy and Daddy wanted her to work in a place where she would meet plenty of eligible young men. Amanda, however, has other ideas — important to her because they are completely opposite to those of her parents. Frankly, I was amused by her efforts to break away from the traditional upper-class upbringing. Apparently her father knew my name and didn't think Amanda would meet the 'right sort of man' in any office of mine!'

Sue laughed.

'My own sister is no better, Ross. It's only ignorance that makes people the way they are. But it's all changing now, isn't it? In another generation's time, the barriers will be down and prejudices with them. It's happening already. Television helps and the mixing up of all classes at schools and universities. We're levelling off, Ross — slowly but surely. It's a good thing basically but I must be honest and admit that I shall regret the loss of some things. The levelling is so often a lowering rather than an elevating, which is sad. You're one of the exceptions to the rule.'

Ross grimaced.

'Am I? Somehow I don't think so. I think the present generation is searching for a set of true values and trying to discard the worthless ones. Youth is fighting for truth and honesty. Like any pendulum, it can swing too far one way or the other. Amanda wants to discard everything to do with her class — or thinks she does. She's too young to see that extremist behaviour doesn't prove anything — rather the reverse.'

'Is she attractive?' The question slipped out unguarded.

A faint smile hovered at the corners of Ross's mouth.

'Yes, she is — but still a child, Sue. I need a woman.'

It was what she had wanted to hear and yet as he paid her the compliment so easily and simply, she felt ashamed. She had no further right to this man's admiration, approval, affection.

'I shall miss you, Ross,' she said quietly. 'We seem to have got to know each other very well in so short a time. I shall miss not being able to talk to you.'

'I regret nothing!' Ross said with sudden violence. 'Only that I have lost you to another man. Nothing else.'

He finished his coffee, and called the waiter over for his bill. Now he seemed to Sue to be in a hurry to leave. He said:

'I expect you want to get back to Paul. I suppose I should be grateful to him for allowing me this last meal with you.'

'I didn't ask for permission. Anyhow Paul isn't in London,' Sue said, her eyes suddenly clouded. 'He's gone home — he lives in the country, in Buckinghamshire. He . . . he won't be back until tomorrow.'

To her surprise, Ross suddenly laughed.

'And to think that for the past half-hour I've been fighting with myself to let you go. Okay — we've still got the whole evening, Sue.' He glanced at his watch and added: 'Only ten o'clock. Let's go somewhere. I'll take you to *Annabel's* and we can dance. Remember we met at a dance? It would be fitting to say goodbye the way we met.'

She hesitated. There was no reason for her to hurry back to her sister's flat. Mary knew she was out with Ross and wouldn't wait up. She would enjoy dancing with him, if that was what he really wanted.

She began:

'I'd love it if . . .'

'Then that's decided. Wait here while I ring up about a table. I think I can fix it. I won't be long.'

An hour later, they were dancing to a Ray Charles old favourite of Sue's — *I Can't Stop Loving You*.

Ross held Sue tightly in his arms. He did not speak. Some of his anguish communicated itself to her and she did not try to pull away when he laid his cheek against hers. It was a curious moment when, without a word spoken, she sensed that he was telling her that he loved her. She, in a strange way, accepted his love — just for these last few hours together.

Ross danced beautifully — moving with surprising lightness and grace for so large a man. She had no difficulty in matching her steps to his and let her thoughts wander dreamily with the music. She could think of Paul now without agony. Tomorrow he would be back in the flat with her. They would be happier than ever before. But tomorrow was a long way off and she was happy tonight with Ross, in the attractive, dimly-lit club, the rhythm of their steps perfectly blending. The melody was sad and romantic. She felt relaxed, at peace, pleasantly tired and languorous.

Ross drank brandy that night. Sue declined

179

another drink so he ordered more coffee for her. Their table was in a quiet corner where they seemed detached from the other guests. Ross sat close, holding her hand. His mood was alternating between intense happiness and abject despair. He knew that this was nothing more than a dream from which, tomorrow, he must wake and face the harsh reality — that he'd lost her for ever. But he tried not to allow himself to think about it. For the moment, she seemed to be completely his.

No! he told himself harshly, not completely. Never again would he hold her cool slender body in his arms; never again see her in the sheer beauty of her nakedness; never again kiss every part of her as he had done that night in La Napoule. Sitting cool and relaxed beside him, Sue could have no idea of the bitter torment of desire he experienced; how he had felt as he held her in his arms on the dance floor, her body soft and supple and at one with his while they moved together to the lilt of that damnably poignant song! He had known this would happen and yet he had still wanted these last hours with her even though part of it was a painful agony of longing. Much of what he felt for her was physical. He wasn't ashamed of it. She had some strange fascination — like a match to spirit — igniting the flame in him with a mere look, a brief touch of her hand, a smile at the corners of her mouth or in her eyes. There could never be a time when he would not desire her. She could do this to him quite unconsciously, and his mind dared not dwell on how he would feel were she deliberately to set out to attract him. He was a little afraid of the intensity of the feelings she aroused in him. Such extremes of emotion were new to him.

When at last she turned to him and said she really ought to go, he felt his heart plunge as though he had received a severe blow. Somehow he had to live through this moment of parting without letting her realise what it cost him.

But he could not summon up the courage to ride home with her in the taxi. Whereas on other occasions he had asked to be allowed to escort her to Mary's flat and she had protested it was too far out of his way, this time he nodded his head.

'Okay, I've paid the driver, Sue. I think you'll be perfectly safe with him.'

'Of course!'

She sat in the back of the taxi, leaning forward on her seat. Ross stood with one foot inside, close to her, watching her intently, bidding her goodbye. He held tightly to her hands. His grip was so intense it was painful. She did not draw away. Suddenly, he was inside the taxi, sitting there on the seat beside her, his arms around her, crushing her against him.

'Goodbye, Sue. Don't forget me!'

His lips were against her mouth, not gently but with a terrible, desperate urgency. Gently, Sue lifted her hand and laid it against his cheek, soothingly as a mother might do to a frightened child.

'Sssh, Ross, don't. Sssh!' she whispered, frightened by his passion and pain and yet wretchedly sensible of its cause.

He drew his lips away and looked down into her eyes with an attempted smile.

'That film we saw together . . . ' his voice was husky. 'Remember the title — 'The Agony And The Ecstasy'? Fits this moment of farewell. Goodbye, my darling.'

The next moment, he was out of the taxi and walking quickly away down the street without a backward glance. Sue felt sudden tears pricking her eyelids.

'Ready to go, Miss?'

She nodded to the taxi driver and sat back against the seat fighting the temptation to cry. There was really nothing to cry about. It had to end and Ross would soon find someone else. He was so very nice . . . many women

182

would fall in love with him. Maybe he would console himself with Amanda, the redhead. Ross had spoken of her as if she were a child but she was eighteen — the same age as Sue, herself, had been when she had first met Paul . . .

'Time I made a woman of you, my little girl!' Paul had said. Maybe Ross would eventually feel that way about Amanda.

Sue tried to fasten her thoughts on the girl who would take the job she had herself so nearly accepted. She tried to remember what Ross had said about her — not a great deal, but for the most part she could think of nothing but a wish which kept repeating itself in the back of her head:

'Be kind to him, Amanda. Don't hurt him. Love him as he needs to be loved.'

11

Paul said:

'You don't seem to be as wildly excited as I'd expected. Not changed your mind, I suppose?'

Sue ran across the room and flung her arms around him.

'I am, I am, Paul. It's the most wonderful news. But I never doubted you'd fix it all — you'd promised you would and I've always had complete faith in you, darling. So it wasn't exactly a surprise.'

He detached her arms from around his neck and stood holding her hands, facing her. He felt faintly irritated.

'You don't seem to realise what a near thing it was, Sue. At first Melanie refused, absolutely and completely refused to contemplate it. It was only at the very last minute she lost her temper and agreed.'

Paul drew Sue over to the sofa and pulled her down beside him.

'I'll tell you about it . . . ' he began but Sue reached up and covered his mouth with her hand.

'No, don't, Paul. I don't want to hear. I

don't even want to think about it. It's enough that . . . that Melanie agreed.'

Paul shrugged.

'Funny little thing you are sometimes, Sue. I'd have thought you'd be avid for the details.' He laughed. 'Don't look so horrified. I didn't mean you were ghoulish, my sweet — merely that you've had this divorce question so much at heart, it would only be natural to want to hear how the result was achieved.'

Sue turned her head away unhappily.

'No, I don't, Paul. I . . . I suppose it's silly but the one part of this I don't like and have always dreaded — is the thought of hurting another woman so badly. I know you say Melanie doesn't love you but it must still be a blow to her pride.'

Again Paul shrugged.

'She doesn't hesitate to undermine other people's pride!' he said bitterly. 'Call it just retribution.'

Sue leaned over and impulsively kissed Paul's mouth. It looked like a sulky thwarted child's.

'Don't let's think about it, darling. Let's just be happy.'

Paul relaxed. He drew her into his arms and kissed her, enjoying the softness and perfume of her skin and silky hair and the beauty of her upcurled lashes.

'Missed me?' he asked softly. 'I wanted you so much last night I nearly came back to the flat. If you'd been here, I would have done but I knew I couldn't go banging on your sister's front door at two in the morning!'

Sue nestled against him, smiling.

'I wasn't there anyway — not until three!' she said dreamily.

Paul stiffened. His reaction surprised her.

'Where the hell were you, then?'

'*Annabel's*. Look, Paul, I told you I was going out with Ross. You said you didn't mind.'

'Like hell! Dinner doesn't mean a whole night's entertainment.'

She refused to take him seriously.

'Don't be so silly, darling!' She leaned back against him but this time he did not put his arms round her so she sat up again. 'Look, Paul, I've said goodbye to Ross. I shall never see him again. It's all over. There's nothing for you to be upset about.'

Paul got up. His face was set — his lips thin.

'Isn't there? I can't see why it should take from seven in the evening until three in the morning for two people to say goodbye. Must have been a very prolonged touching farewell. If it was all that difficult for you to ditch him there must have been more in it for you than I realised.'

Sue gasped. She had never known Paul to be jealous before. But of course there had never been any occasion when he had been put to the test. In all the seven years they had shared, she had never gone out with another man; or given a second look to any one Paul introduced. There were not many. Paul had wanted to keep her apart from his colleagues as well as from family friends who might report back to Melanie. Paul's behaviour now astonished more than upset her.

She stood up and went to him. Ignoring his taught body, she put her arms around him.

'Darling, I'm in love with *you*. Isn't that all that matters?'

'No, it damn well isn't. Did you ever sleep with him?'

She went scarlet — and felt helplessly angry about that tell-tale colour.

'I don't see that what happened after I left you is in the least important now.' Her voice was hurried, uncertain.

'So you did! You were unfaithful — while I was eating my heart out for you. I think it's horrible, Sue — rather disgusting in fact.'

She felt as though he had hit her.

'Oh, Paul, darling, *please*! You don't understand. I was eating my heart out, too. I thought I'd never see you again. Ross came on the scene and I was so lonely . . . so miserable . . . well — I didn't *make* it happen — it just happened.'

'But you didn't object!' It was more an accusation than a question. Sue turned away uneasily. She wanted to put an end to this unexpected quarrel — Paul *must* see that he had no cause to be jealous of Ross — yet she could not truthfully say that she had raised objections to Ross's love-making.

'Well?'

She felt confused — uncertain now of herself.

'Paul, I love *you*. No one in the whole world matters to me but you. Don't let's think about the past. You asked me often enough in the old days not to think about your wife; told me that what you did with *her* wasn't important to us. What happened between Ross and me wasn't important either — at least, not to me; not now we're together again. You don't have to concern yourself about Ross, Paul. I love you, *you*!'

He was finally convinced, caught up by the passion in her voice as much as by the warm surrender of her young body pressed against his. He caught her face between his hands and kissed her quickly, deeply, bruising her lips.

'You're mine, mine!' he said possessively, and his fingers began to pull at the zip of her dress. 'I made you mine and I'm keeping you mine.'

There was no seduction this time in his love-making. He took her fiercely, even a little cruelly but she submitted to it, swept away in the tide of his passion, curiously aware at the time that the desire was Paul's rather than hers. She even welcomed this new impatience in Paul believing it to be an increased love for her. She was happy that he should have forgotten Ross. Now she would forget him, too.

But when it was over and they lay exhausted in each other's arms, Paul said suddenly:

'Was he better than me?'

She felt a shock of surprise mixed with dismay. She tried to answer but failed. Paul took her chin in his hand and turned her face so that he could look in her eyes.

'Was he? *Was he?*'

She pulled herself out of his arms and began to reach for her clothes.

'It never occurred to me to make comparisons,' she said and her voice was suddenly harsh, 'It's rather a horrid question, Paul — one you had no right to ask.'

'No right? When I'm going to marry you?

Haven't I a right to know about your past affairs?'

She was suddenly hurt and angry.

'No, Paul, no right. I don't ask you how it is for you with Melanie. Would you like me to enquire if she excites you more than I do? I assume because you have chosen to live with me, that it is me you love. Sex is surely only a part of the whole world of our love and loving. Ross isn't *important* . . . I love you. I think that is all you need to know, isn't it?'

He walked past her into the bathroom. His eyes were veiled, unfriendly. When he came out, he said:

'I take it then that you found Bryant a better lover than me. Otherwise you would have denied it.'

She turned on him furiously.

'You're mad and I think it would be wrong — even indecent of me to discuss what happened with Ross. Unfair to *him*.'

'So you think it's fair to me to let me wonder all the time if I'm inadequate?'

Her anger suddenly vanished. She held out a hand and smiled.

'Darling, do let's stop this. It's silly. Would I be back here with you if I found you inadequate as a lover?'

'But you aren't living here with me. You're still living with that ghastly sister of yours.'

190

'Not any more, Paul. When I go home tonight, I'll tell her about the divorce. I'll move my things back here. Tomorrow — okay?'

He nodded, lighting a cigarette. Sue felt a momentary disappointment. Paul was giving in with a poor grace. Strange to say it made him seem younger than herself. Until now, she had been the immature one, Paul the sophisticated teacher. Now in some subtle way she did not understand, the balance of their relationship had changed.

When she went out of the room into the kitchen to make a salad for their lunch, she found herself quite unwittingly pondering the question Paul had put to her. *Was Ross a better lover?* Or was it just that Ross always tried to please *her* — all the giving on his side? Paul could be a selfish lover, impatient with the slower feminine tempo, lacking tolerance if, as on several occasions, acute fatigue or an emotional scene affected her responses. Paul believed that to make love was the best and only way to end a disagreement. He could not see that it was Sue's state of mind that affected her desire. But those occasions had been rare. It was Paul of course, who had taught her all about sex. No living human being knew as much about her as he did. She could not fully understand his jealousy of Ross when he knew that he, Paul, was the only man she could ever really love and belong to.

Paul seemed in a better mood during lunch. He extracted a firm promise from her that she would not let Mary deflect her from returning to the flat tomorrow. For good, this time, Paul added with mock severity. No running away a second time — his nerves would not stand the strain. They parted on the best, most affectionate terms.

Sue knew that Mary would make things as difficult as possible. But she was not prepared for the full force of her sister's outburst.

'You are out of your mind. You told me nothing would make you go back to the hell of your life with Paul. Have you forgotten what it was like?'

Sue argued:

'His wife has agreed to a divorce, Mary. Paul wants to marry me. You just don't seem to understand.'

Mary looked at her sister pityingly.

'You are the one who doesn't understand. So Paul tells you his wife has agreed to a divorce. *How do you know it's the truth?* He'd do anything to get you back. And even if she has agreed, how do you know she'll stick to the agreement? *And* even if the divorce goes through, how can you be sure he'll marry you at the end of it? How you can stand there and say you trust him after what he has done to you, I just don't know. Good God, I'd rather you'd told me you were going to live with that new boy friend of yours.'

Sue found her suitcases and began to pack. Mary sat on the bed watching her. Sue felt nervous and anxious to be gone. She could see the anger and reproach in her sister's eyes.

'Don't do it, Sue. Can't you see, this is all the wrong way? Why, if he loves you, can't you wait until the divorce is through before you go back to live with him? What's got into you? You admitted to me he was no good; that he never meant to marry you. Why do you believe he has changed all that much? Your only hope is to stay away from him until he's free to marry you. Once you're living with him again, there'll be no need for him to get a divorce, will there?'

Her face white, Sue turned on Mary at last.

'Paul knows that I won't live with him indefinitely as I used to do. But I'm not going to use blackmail on him, Mary. It could be months, years before the divorce is finalised. Paul and I don't want to be apart that long, do we? We love each other. Don't you understand?'

'Oh, yes, I understand that you think you

love him. But I can't accept that *he* loves *you* — not after the way he treated you. I don't see how you can trust him, Sue. Maybe you don't. Maybe that's why you are going back to him — to make sure he doesn't find someone else.'

Sue began to tremble, all her nerves on edge.

'Mary, for God's sake. I'm twenty-four. Let me lead my own life — for better or for worse. I can't explain — I just know that I *have* to go back to Paul. I just have to, Mary. That's all. Isn't it enough?'

Mary twisted angrily on the bed.

'Not for me, it isn't. I can see the future, Sue — which is more than you seem able to do. In ten years you'll be saying the same things to me and the only difference will be that even you don't believe them any longer. It'll be too late then by far for any other man. Do, *do*, please reconsider, Sue. I'm not suggesting you stop seeing him. I only ask that you don't go back to live with him until his divorce is through. See him every day if you must, sleep with him if you must, but don't live with him.'

A little unnerved finally by the urgency and appeal in her sister's voice, Sue, in turn, appealed again for understanding.

'I don't see what difference there is

between seeing him and sleeping with him, as you put it, and actually living under the same roof with him. I know Melanie can name me in the case and I don't mind. It would happen anyway, wouldn't it? She may already have all the evidence she needs.'

Mary held out a desperate hand.

'It isn't your good name I'm worrying about now,' she cried. 'It's your future happiness. You cannot afford to trust Paul. Once he has you back with him, there's no need for him to get this divorce.'

'That's absurd. He knows I'd leave him again if he went back on his word.'

'Does he? And would you? It took seven years for you to get up the courage last time. How long this time, Sue? Another seven?'

Wearily, Sue turned away, bent down and fastened the locks on her suitcase.

'I don't expect you to trust Paul, or me,' she said drily. 'Just try not to worry about me, Mary. I'm sorry I can't do as you ask but I can't. Paul needs me and I'm going to him.'

To Sue's horror, Mary burst into tears.

Speaking of it later to Paul, Sue herself was near to tears.

'I couldn't convince her it was going to be all right. I've never seen her go to pieces before. It was awful, Paul, awful!'

Paul held her in his arms, his face uneasy

and not a little disconcerted.

'She never did like me, did she? I suppose I can't blame her. Try to forget it, Sue. She'll get over it.'

He made love to her. For a little while, she did indeed forget her sister's distraught face but the memory returned when the love-making was over. She had not realised how fond Mary was of her, nor how much her sister's opinion mattered to her. She was much more deeply affected by Mary's prophecies than she cared to think. She tried hard to keep her mind on Paul; to think how attentive he was; how loving and how passionately they had just made love. But at the same time she could not push out of her mind the fact that Paul had not mentioned Melanie or the divorce again.

She told herself she was being unreasonable. She had made it clear to Paul she didn't want to be given the details. If he told her nothing more, it was by her own request. And if she wanted information, she had only to ask. But she could not bring herself to do this. Paul might think she didn't trust him and she did. *She did.*

Suddenly, the insecurity of her position frightened her. If Paul let her down, she had no one to turn to. She couldn't go back to Mary and Joe — pride would never permit it.

She had cut herself off from all her friends, her family, even Ross.

Quickly, she shook herself out of such stupid apprehension. Paul had promised; Melanie had agreed. It was only Mary's tearful forebodings which were responsible for this foolish gloomy mood.

She went over to Paul and rubbed her cheek against his shoulder.

'We're going to be very happy, aren't we, darling?' she said softly.

Paul stared at her with surprise:

'Aren't we happy now?' he asked.

12

Mary sat beside her sister on the soft cushioned sofa and looked at her over the rim of her sherry glass.

'Well — well! I must say you look fine, Sue.'

Sue sipped her own drink and laughed contentedly — eyes shining — lips confident.

'What did you expect, you old pessimist? I am happy, Mary. And I think it's wonderful of you to come. I know how you feel about Paul . . . ' She broke off, unable to express her full emotions. Somehow Mary coming here to the flat, willing to meet Paul, be friendly with him meant so much more than she could ever know. It was almost as though Mary were saying: *I was wrong, you were right — Paul does love you; does mean to marry you.* It was like a family blessing, somehow, Sue thought whimsically.

She wasn't sure what had prompted Mary to come. The sisters had exchanged no word since Sue's departure three weeks earlier. Then came Mary's unexpected telephone call yesterday saying she would come and see Sue if she would like it, some time after tea the next day. Sue was amazed to find how much she wanted to be in touch with her sister again.

Of course, Paul did not understand Sue's radiant smiles when she told him about the reunion. His handsome face seemed to grow suddenly hard.

'What's the point? Mary doesn't like me and never will. Personally, I'd rather she didn't come to our place. She's only hoping to find you down-trodden and miserable!'

Sue laughed and touched his cheek with her finger, tenderly. She was too happy to protest. Laughing, she told Paul not to be so mean. Mary was offering the olive branch. The least he could do if he loved *her*, was to accept it with good grace.

But Paul continued to look hard and to be uncooperative.

'Well, I'm not rushing home early! I'll leave you both to a long sisterly gossip, and come back just as she's going.'

Sue remembered that as she sat with Mary today. She looked at her watch. Six-thirty. Paul ought to be here soon. She was impatient for him to come. When Mary saw him, talked to him, realised to the full, his devotion and loyalty to her, she'd be more understanding. She wouldn't want to deny her such happiness. And Paul would realise that underneath her brusque exterior, Mary had a heart of gold.

The elder sister sighed as she watched the changing expressions of Sue's beautiful face. She felt only misgivings. Sue was so transparent. It must be child's play for a clever man like Paul Manton to know how to deal with her and twist her round his little finger. Anyone could see that she was in a fever of impatience this very moment. He would see at once that she had been waiting for him — longing for him. Poor infatuated Sue!

Mary was in no hurry for Paul to come. She was here entirely against her better judgment for she felt she would never be able to pretend to like Paul, no matter how happy Sue seemed to be. She was here only because that man, Ross Bryant, had put the fear of God into her . . . even into Joe.

Despite herself, Mary suddenly smiled. It was impossible not to like Ross — he was so completely without guile — so genuine. He was incapable of dissembling or hypocrisy. He certainly never tried to hide the fact that he was crazy about Sue — and so it was all too easy to believe that his fears for her had foundation. And he had been full of them. He had said:

'Suppose she isn't happy? Suppose he's let

her down and she's all alone? You know your sister — she's proud; she won't ask for help a second time, from you or from me. I can't do anything, but you could — you could get in touch with her; find out if she's all right. Can't you just do that? I'm worried. Surely you must be too.'

'Phone calls, one after the other, and finally Ross had called to see them. Strangely enough he and Joe had got on like a house on fire, and over all the many drinks, he'd started to tackle Joe about his sister-in-law.

'Someone's got to look after Sue. She's incapable of taking care of herself. Surely you don't trust that bastard she's living with? She's part of your family. You must be concerned about her. No one's heard a word from her since she went back to him.'

'Well, why don't you go round?' Joe finally asked his wife. 'I can't poke my nose in but you could.'

Later, privately, he had said laughing: 'At least it will stop that crazy fellow from pestering the life out of us. He's right, too, of course. We ought to keep some kind of tabs on Sue. He's dead right. She's cracked — always has been about Paul Manton — needs someone to steady the boat. You go, Mary.'

So here she was, rather unbelievably,

because Ross Bryant had made her come here. He was sick with worry about Sue. It was a bit ironic — and grim. The humour of the situation disappeared when one considered that tomorrow she would probably have to report to him that Sue was perfectly all right; as much in love with her Paul as ever; and, according to her, confidently awaiting the promised divorce. She would have to tell Ross his fears for Sue were groundless. In a way he'd be glad — but would he be disappointed, too?

The thought seemed mean. Whatever else was in doubt, she certainly believed Ross loved Sue and that his love was of the unselfish kind. Oh, no doubt he'd be pleased, relieved and delighted to know Sue was happy.

The shrill bell of Sue's telephone rang. She picked up the receiver and with her hand covering the mouth-piece, whispered to Mary: 'Hope it isn't Paul to say he's hung up at the office.'

But it wasn't Paul. *It was Melanie, his wife.*

'Perhaps you didn't hear about the accident — it was on the six o'clock news. You'd better tell Paul to ring me the moment he gets in. There'll be all kinds of things he'll have to attend to. The lawyers have been on to me already — you see, with his uncle and cousin

202

both dead, Paul becomes Sir Paul Manton. Kindly tell him to ring me at once, will you?'

Sue hardly spoke. She replaced the receiver, her hand shaking. It was the first time she had ever spoken to Paul's wife. The cool, remote voice, slightly disdainful, had shaken her badly. She didn't fully understand what it was all about. Obviously someone important in Paul's family had met with sudden death. Sue tried hard to remember all she knew about his relatives but could only recall an elderly uncle and aunt who lived in Australia, or was it South Africa? And a son — Paul's cousin. Were these titled? She couldn't remember Paul saying so.

Mary was unable to offer any constructive suggestions. She knew nothing of Paul's background other than that he came of a good family but had little money of his own. Sue had told her that Melanie had all the money. Apprehensive, subdued, the sisters waited for Paul's arrival.

He came in ten minutes later looking flushed and not quite as smooth or debonair as usual. His lips were sulky. He went straight to Sue, and ignored Mary.

'Sorry to mess up the party but I'm afraid I have to go home at once. They caught me on the 'phone just as I was leaving the office. Uncle Godfrey — Sir Godfrey Manton

— was killed this afternoon when the helicopter he was in crashed into some trees. My cousin, Giles, too. Giles was his heir. I never expected that I . . . '

He broke off biting his lips and turned apologetically to Mary.

'Please excuse me — things are a bit tricky.'

Mary acknowledged this with a nod.

Sue looked at Paul anxiously.

'Your wife 'phoned. She said you were needed — that you would have to go home at once.'

'Yes. I spoke to Melanie. She told me.' He put his arm round Sue's shoulder. 'Sorry, darling,' he added. 'It's all a bit of a mess. I'll have to go down and sort everything out. I really am sorry. I'll come back as soon as I can — a day or two at the most. Be an angel and pack a night-bag for me, will you? I must order a taxi — might just catch the seven-five if I hurry.'

'Would you like me to leave you two alone?' Mary asked, but Sue shook her head.

'No, please stay if you can. I'll want someone to talk to after Paul has gone.'

She went into the bedroom and began to pack a bag for Paul. She could hear him in the bathroom using his electric shaver. She paused as she was about to put a pair of white silk pyjamas into the case. Her eyes filled with sudden tears. Paul came to the doorway and shot her a speculative look.

'You do understand, don't you? There's no need for you to upset yourself, Sue.'

She turned away quickly and continued packing.

'I suppose you do have to go, Paul? I mean home — ' she hated that word. Paul's home was here, surely, with her in the flat. 'Can't you see the lawyers and so on here, in town?'

Paul switched off his electric razor in order to hear her better. He shrugged his shoulders a little impatiently.

'Don't be awkward, darling. Of course I must go home. I can't deal with such an important personal affair at my office and you must see for yourself I can't deal with it here. It's not as if you were my wife . . . yet!'

He saw Sue flinch and the glisten of tears on her long lashes. He went across and put an arm around her, and laid a freshly-shaven cheek against her wet one.

'Darling! You're not jealous, surely? You must know very well by now that I haven't the slightest desire to see Melanie or go back to that damned house. But I've got to. It's purely business — nothing more.'

She managed to smile up at him.

'I know. I'm being silly. Forgive me?'

He kissed her quickly, patted her shoulder

and wandered back into the bathroom to collect sponge-bag and razor.

He was obviously in a hurry to be off. She could see that. But he spared time for a quick drink and to explain to Sue and Mary that he'd never given much thought to either of these dead relatives whom he had never met. Sir Godfrey Manton, Bart., was his father's older brother. He had emigrated to South Africa between the two world wars. Paul's cousin was Sir Godfrey's immediate heir. After him, Paul's father would have inherited but he had died. It had rarely occurred to Paul that he might one day inherit either title or money. His cousin Giles was younger than he, and there was no reason to expect an early demise. But with Sir Godfrey and Giles wiped out in one fatal accident, Paul was sole heir to the title and the estate in South Africa. As far as Paul knew this consisted of an enormous farm near Johannesburg — a very valuable property.

'Lady Manton — my Aunt Sheila, is presumably still alive and will have to be supported. Somewhere at the back of my mind, I'm sure I heard that old Uncle Godfrey was a bit of a lad and believed in *la dolce vita*. He had spent a lot of his money on gambling. I'm not anticipating much beyond the title and a load of worries. Pity!

We could do with some cash just now, couldn't we, darling?' he added, smiling at Sue. She began to feel better and gave his hand a quick squeeze.

'You know I don't care about that,' she said softly.

After Paul left, Sue told her sister that she had at last lined up a job which would bring in nearly seven thousand a year.

'Even though Paul may have to pay Melanie alimony and support his son, we should be able to manage quite comfortably on our two incomes,' she announced.

Mary followed her into the small kitchen and watched Sue put a steak under the grill. Mary had promised to stay and eat Paul's share. She would 'phone Joe. He'd understand. Sue's finances were not Mary's worry, but what if she and Paul started a family? Sooner or later, Sue would want children. Then . . . somehow it was impossible to imagine the man-about-town Paul, denying himself in order to support a child.

'You don't really know Paul!' Sue kept saying. Her eyes were soft with love. 'He'll give up anything for me, Mary. You can see he doesn't care a damn about this title. There may be no more ski-ing holidays or summer trips abroad. Melanie used to finance all the luxuries. Paul's used to them. It won't be easy for him to think in terms of cheap hotels and various economies which he'll have to practise if there's no money with this title. He says he doesn't mind being poor so long as he's with me. Sometimes I feel I've no right to expect him to give up so much for me. I hope he does inherit some money from his uncle, not for me, for *him*.'

'Don't be silly, Sue!' Mary said more sharply than she had intended. 'Paul isn't the only one to be giving up a few luxuries. You might have married Ross Bryant and lived in the lap of luxury for the rest of *your life*.'

Sue raised her eyebrows.

'You know I never even contemplated marrying Ross — much as I liked him.'

'But he wanted to marry you. You might have had all you wanted.'

Sue smiled.

'I happen only to want Paul and you surprise me, Mary. There was a time when you were against my even knowing Ross. You're surely not so mercenary that you're beginning to think his money is more important than his background?'

Mary flushed and frowned as she stubbed out her cigarette. She had given Ross her word that she would not divulge the fact that he and she had been in touch and that it was really at his instigation she was here now. At the same time, she felt the need to champion him.

'We're not all of us right all the time,' she said rather pompously, 'I've thought things over and admit I was wrong about Ross. I don't think his background *does* matter. Not because he has money although that undoubtedly helps to sweep away a few class-barriers — but because he's so nice. He's genuinely in love with you, Sue.'

Now Sue felt a jab of uneasy remembrance. The memory of Ross's eyes — his arms — his tender care of her. She said:

'I know, Mary. I feel guilty about Ross. I'm afraid I hurt him, though I never wanted to. I liked him — very, very much. I admired his wonderful qualities of kindness and generosity. But I wasn't in love with him. I think I just needed the care he gave me then. Wherever he is, I hope he'll be happy. I want everybody to be as happy as I am. Oh, Mary, surely you have changed your mind about Paul, too? Admit you were wrong about him. Admit that he isn't the selfish monster you thought him. You can see for yourself how much he loves me and how happy we are now.'

'Sometimes, Sue, I find your touching faith in Paul a bit sick-making. You're *too* childishly credulous.'

At once Sue was up in arms, flushed and indignant.

'If you're going to start being nasty about Paul again . . . '

'I'm not, I'm not,' broke in Mary, 'but you just won't be realistic. You're so hopelessly romantic. Take this new situation. Aren't you scared that Paul has now inherited a baronetcy and perhaps a fortune?'

'There probably is no fortune. Paul said his uncle gambled most of it away. He'll probably only inherit a pile of bills and an old aunt who will have to be financed. She's been in a Home for years with some sort of wasting disease.'

'But Paul's got a title now,' Mary persisted, 'and his wife might enjoy being My Lady.'

'I refuse to let you get me down!' Sue exclaimed, and looked at her sister angrily.

'Oh, very well,' said Mary shrugging, 'let's drop the subject.'

'I mean to. I don't think the title will make the slightest difference to Paul or his intention to leave Melanie and marry me.'

Mary renewed her former friendliness.

'Look, Sue, why don't you come back to us for the night? With Paul away . . . ?'

Sue hesitated. She didn't really want to spend the night alone but Paul might have urgent news and ring her. He would worry if there was no reply — maybe even get that silly idea back in his head that she was out with Ross Bryant — was starting that affair up again. She wouldn't risk such a thing.

'No, I won't come, but thanks for asking me. I'll ring you tomorrow, Mary, and let you know what's happening,' she said.

The sisters parted later that evening on affectionate terms.

Sue walked into the deserted sitting-room and tried not to feel the shadow of sudden loneliness.

She felt sure somehow that Paul would ring later.

She switched on the television. She tried to concentrate on the programme but couldn't. She turned it off — feeling depressed and troubled.

At ten o'clock, she went to bed with a book but failed to concentrate. At midnight she put out the light and closed her eyes. She tossed sleeplessly on her pillow. She knew that now it was too late for Paul to ring, and that she must get through the night before she could once again start listening for the telephone; to hear Paul's reassuring voice telling her he was on his way back.

13

Paul crossed his legs and leaned back against the cushions, cupping the big round brandy glass in both hands. He sipped the Cognac appreciatively. It was perfect, following the wonderful dinner Melanie had just given him . . . a gourmet's meal. Of course, Melanie hadn't cooked it — merely ordered it and left the excellent girl to do the work. But the choice of dishes had been hers and the menu as always, was cleverly chosen: his favourite caviar; the duckling with orange sauce; the fresh peaches.

The brandy, too, was from one of the vintage bottles usually reserved for V.I.P.'s. Melanie wanted particularly to impress.

Watch it, Paul told himself cynically; Melanie must want something pretty badly.

He glanced at her over the rim of his glass. She was standing with one elbow resting on the mantelpiece, the arm raised so that the curve of her small pointed breast stood out in sharp relief. She wore a very short tight-fitting black skirt that curved under her buttocks and clung to her slim thighs, just as the soft chiffon blouse with the wide frills clung to her rounded shoulders and bosom. She looked utterly feminine, and highly sophisticated. She stood still, not looking in his direction but holding a tiny gold-rimmed coffee cup in her free hand. Her nails were long, pointed and silvered. She was using a new pale make-up and pale, glistening lip-stick.

She turned her head suddenly and he looked quickly away, embarrassed to be caught staring at her. A smile curved her mouth.

'Well, Paul, nice to have you home!'

He glanced at the ash on the end of his cigar and made no reply. He wasn't going to make the obvious reply that he found it 'nice to be home'.

'You know, Paul, I do believe I've put on weight!' came from Melanie suddenly.

Startled, he looked up just in time to see her hand running with deliberate sensuousness over her breasts down to the gently-curving hip bones, and lingering on her thighs. He looked quickly away. It was true — she did seem less angular; softer, as if her figure had filled out and increased her feminine allure. He'd often told her she should put on weight.

She laughed, startling him; then came over and sat down beside him, letting her hand rest with a merest suggestion of a touch on his knee. He felt his muscle jump. His annoyance increased. He had no intention of being fooled by Melanie's mood.

'What is it you want?' he asked in a rough voice and finished his Cognac.

'*Want*? Why, Paul, what a question. Who could want anything more after a meal like that? I must say Carmela does us proud, doesn't she? I think I really will have to put up her wages, or my dear friend Lady Bartley will try and bribe her away. She adores Carmela's cooking.'

She removed her hand from Paul's knee and touched his chin.

'Why, darling, I think *you're* thinner. Yes, you are. I can see I shall have to feed you up.'

Paul jerked his face away.

'How's the boy?' he asked abruptly.

'Matt? Oh, he's fine. I didn't keep him up — he was so tired, poor sweet. But you'll see him in the morning. I told him Daddy was coming back from his holiday and he was absolutely thrilled. You should have . . .'

'Melanie, I've hardly been on a holiday,' broke in Paul, his face tense. 'I think it's wrong to let the boy suppose I'm going to stay.'

'But Paul, you *are* staying, surely? You're

not trying to say this is only a quick visit after all that has happened?'

He looked at her and his sharp anger was deflected by the glint of amusement somewhere in the back of her eyes.

'I don't know what you're up to, Melanie, but let's get this straight — I'm home this evening purely on business — nothing more. I shall leave as soon as Uncle Godfrey's affairs are cleared up.'

Melanie laughed.

'Oh, don't be silly, darling. Of course you'll do no such thing. You don't think for one moment I'd agree to you rushing away again now I've got you back. Why, it's absurd. You've just been away for three weeks — surely you can spend a little time in your own home, no matter how tempting your temptations are ... ' Melanie gave her throaty little laugh.

Paul clenched his fist.

'You're being deliberately obtuse, Melanie. Anyone would think you'd forgotten we are in the process of getting divorced.'

Melanie's dark eyebrows were now two sharply curved wings over her heavily shadowed eyes.

'*Divorced*? Are you mad, Paul? You surely didn't take our stupid row seriously!'

Paul's mouth fell open. Now she really had

succeeded in getting below the skin. He exploded.

'I damn well did. You're not trying to tell me you didn't go to Mr Tanner that Monday morning? You promised you would. You agreed that you'd see your own solicitor and set the ball rolling. You said . . . '

'For heaven's sake, Paul, stop being so stupid,' she cut in. 'Of course I did no such thing. We've had rows before and neither of us has taken them seriously. Of course I didn't see Mr Tanner. What an idea! Paul, darling! . . . ' Her tone changed and became gentle, coaxing. 'Don't pretend that all these weeks you've been imagining some ghastly old detective was going to pop in on you and your girlfriend and collect the dreadful evidence. Poor Sweet — no wonder you look half dead! Well, put your mind at rest — no such thing happened, or ever will. I haven't said one word against you to Mr Tanner.'

'Melanie . . . ' Paul broke off, unable to find words to cope with his anger, his confusion, his sense of anti-climax and beneath it all, just the first tiny twinge of relief.

She swung her feet off the floor and tucking them beneath her, leaned closer to his shoulder. He stayed rigid at her side, his brows drawn down, his mouth tightening in the effort to remain calm. He could smell that fascinating perfume 'Georgio' she always used and could see all too clearly in his mind's eye the creamy beauty of the small firm breast now touching his arm.

'I do credit you with a little intelligence, Paul,' she was saying. 'I know we both say things in the heat of the moment, but once I'd calmed down, I realised you couldn't possibly have meant what you said. You couldn't really want to leave me — or our son.'

'I did mean it. I'm in love with Sue and I . . .'

'Oh, I know all about her,' broke in Melanie smoothly, 'I don't blame you. I'm honest enough to admit I drove you to be unfaithful to me. I was horrid. It was all my fault.'

'All your fault?' She really had succeeded in surprising him now. Never in all their years together had Melanie admitted that *she* was in the wrong.

'But of course, darling. I wasn't quite as . . . well, keen about bed as you . . . it stood to reason you'd look elsewhere . . . it's the usual reason why a husband looks for fun and games outside his own home. But I quite made up my mind about that side of our marriage. From now on, we're going to have

217

the perfect sex life. It isn't as though I am frigid, Paul. You very well know I enjoy it just as much as you but we rather let it develop into a battle of wits, didn't we? Well, from now on, things will be different — I'll be carefree and natural about it all. We'll make love when we feel like it — *now*, if you like. I must say I feel like it. You're so annoyingly masculine, Paul . . . I can't ignore you the way I'd like to. You know, darling, I always did find you the most attractive man in the world.'

Her voice was low, husky, seductive. He fought against it; fought against the tell-tale stirring of his senses and knew that it was a losing battle. His body, if not his mind, was already betraying his desire. She could be irresistible — she knew it. Her hand reached down at the same time as her mouth, soft, moist and warm, pressed against his.

He breathed hard, his whole body tense.

'Damn you, *damn you!*' he whispered, then his lips opened against hers — searching, demanding, appealing. His hands reached out of their own volition to touch those perfect breasts and as his fingers found the remembered curves, he realised that she was wearing nothing under the filmy blouse. She had deliberately intended to seduce him.

'*Damn you!*' he said again savagely, and

gentleness was lost in a new fury that became total surrender. His eyes opened suddenly and saw hers open, too, sparkling with laughter, with a triumph that told him more surely than ever, that he was lost, *lost* for evermore in the hot sweet jungle darkness of her.

When they found breath again to speak, Melanie's voice was as feline as the relaxed softness of her replete and satisfied body.

'Know what, Paul? Even if I had started divorce proceedings, this would mean I condoned your infidelities. So we're back to square one, my darling.'

'Ummm!' He couldn't yet trust his voice. He didn't trust her, either. Any moment, she might turn back into the old hard cruel Melanie who could taunt him, fill him with desire and hope and fling it all away with fantastic heartlessness.

'Know what else? We didn't take care. Just suppose . . . ' she broke off on a subtle, significant little laugh.

He tried not to follow her thought but the shock registered. Still he could not let her go. He went on caressing her — possessing her warm, perfumed body.

'And something else, Paul darling . . . ' she kissed him slowly and carefully, her lips lingering on his mouth, 'any moment, Bates will be in for the coffee cups!'

This time he did sit up, hurriedly straightening his clothing. Melanie's chiffon blouse was open, her body naked and seemingly unashamed, exposed for Bates as well as for her husband to see.

'Cover up — ' he began, but seeing the laughter in her eyes, dropped to his knees and kissed her quickly on each pink raised nipple, 'No, don't cover *them*, don't!'

But she moved away after a moment and said gently:

'Never mind. There's always later!'

She rearranged her clothing and her hair, brought him another glass of brandy, and sat down opposite him, her legs crossed primly at the ankles, her hands neatly folded in her lap.

'All ready for Bates!' she said.

As if on cue, the butler came in. He took the coffee tray and turned to Melanie.

'Anything more you require, Madam?'

Her mouth twitched.

'No, thank, you, Bates. I've had all I want for the moment!'

They restrained their laughter until the man had gone. Between gasps, Paul said:

'You're incorrigible. What's come over you, Melanie? You've changed.'

She gave him a quick sideways glance.

'Of course. It isn't every day one inherits a

title, my darling. Lady Manton — sounds respectable. I intend to behave respectably from now on. You, too, Sir Paul!'

'Respectably!' Paul echoed, 'My God, Melanie, you astonish me. Suppose Bates *had* come in earlier?'

'Then he'd have learned rather late in life about the birds and the bees!' Melanie began to put more colour on her lips. 'As a matter of fact, he's so well trained, he'd probably have picked up the tray and walked straight out again without speaking to us.'

Paul was thinking again.

'Being Lady Manton — is that what has changed you, Melanie? Towards me, I mean — the idea of the title?'

The teasing look went from her eyes. She said evenly:

'Maybe. I certainly don't intend to miss out on it, Paul. Why should I? I've always been just as ambitious as you and never tried to pretend otherwise. I'm not ashamed of it. It will suit me very well to be Her Ladyship. I like the idea. It'll help you in your job, too. It always helps. The world is still full of snobs. Besides, I've no one else I particularly wish to live with. I think we're extraordinarily well suited, you and I, as a matter of fact.'

'At least that's honest. But it isn't quite so simple for me — there's still Sue . . . '

Melanie yawned.

'Don't be old-fashioned, Paul. I'm not beefing about her or throwing down ultimatums about you never seeing her again. If you must have a mistress, have *her*. I don't care. She seems tame and manageable. Anyway, you won't need a mistress if I'm nice to you — will you? You must sort things out for yourself, my darling. But for heaven's sake, do it *unemotionally*. You know you'd absolutely *loathe* being poor. So would I. We're neither of us cut out for love at the kitchen sink. Besides, you know as well as I do you aren't really in love with this girl. You've known her for years, haven't you? If you'd really been in love you'd have left me for her ages ago. And you certainly wouldn't have made love to me just now in *that* way!'

Paul bit his lip. Melanie's honest appraisal of the facts was pretty brutal — and, as so often — horribly near the truth. If he'd really wanted to marry Sue, he would have broken away from Melanie at the very beginning. But he hadn't wanted to marry her. *Sue* was the one who insisted on marriage. His own marriage suited him very well. Melanie was right. It was only at Sue's insistent demand that he'd decided on divorce.

'Then there's your career to think about,' Melanie went on. 'Your name is bound to attract publicity for a while to come — you can't possibly live openly with her. You must see that. And Matt needs you. You've got to consider him. He's in line for the baronetcy now. So even if you had really meant me to divorce you, you can't go ahead with it now. Do you know, I've had two daily and one Sunday newspaper on to me already asking for 'exclusives'. I told them you were abroad but would be coming home. I was scared stiff someone would put them on to your flat.'

Paul felt suddenly cold. He stood up and walked over to the fireplace. Melanie wasn't mincing matters. He supposed he ought to be grateful to her for the way in which she was discussing the situation so honestly. She wasn't being hysterical or emotional now — merely one hundred percent practical. He, too, must try to think unemotionally. Melanie was so right about publicity and the boy, Matt. Yet he must think, too, of what this would do to Sue. She trusted him. He'd promised her. He'd be the worst kind of bastard to let her down after all the years of love and devotion she'd given him. He couldn't do it to her. She would never forgive him. What would she do with her life? How could he face her with the actual words . . . 'I've got to leave you'.

He could send her a letter maybe — the

coward's way; tell her she could stay on in the flat until she had somewhere else to go. Perhaps that sister of hers would offer her a home again. She'd have to see things from his point of view as well as her own. He couldn't invite gossip now by continuing to live openly with her. Anyway, Melanie had said she wouldn't consider divorcing him now. He had no grounds on which to divorce her, even if he wanted to do so. When Sue got over the first shock, she'd realise that everything had changed and probably for the best. It was not his fault.

Suddenly he realised that he was no longer thinking in terms of what he *might* do, but of how Sue would react when he did what must now be done. His mind was already made up. He only needed the guts to go through with it.

'Paul, why don't you let me go and see the girl?' he heard his wife asking him. 'Maybe woman to woman I could make her see that it's the kindest thing she can do — to give you up. If she really loves you, she'll want what is best for you, won't she? I could make her see that. It would be much more difficult for you.'

Paul gave Melanie a long, appraising stare:

'I didn't realise you cared for me so much!' he said with an edge of sarcasm.

'Oh, I care, darling — about you and that title. I'm not pretending it hasn't made a difference. Nor will you, if you're absolutely honest about it. It's served to widen the gap between the two alternatives open to you. Stay with me. I've got the money. You've got the title. See your career prospects soar, or go to her and watch them collapse. It's that simple now. And I shall never divorce you Paul, whatever you decide. I want you as much if not more than she does. I really do. You, not just the title, darling.'

Her hand clung to his. He wanted to believe her. In a way, he did believe her. Melanie had always been honest. If he was to cut Sue out of his life, then he would need Melanie far more than he had done in the past. She was the perfect hostess for him and if Melanie really meant to put their sex life on a different basis . . .

'Darling, don't look so tormented,' she whispered against his ear, 'You don't have to make any earth-moving decisions tonight. Besides, it's getting late and I'm ready for . . . bed?'

There was the barest hesitation before the last word; the merest rising inflexion. Paul felt his pulses quicken. Melanie always had been able to rouse him as no other woman could — she could be cruel, hard and tormenting but she was all woman and when she wanted, she gave back as much as she took.

She came across to him slowly, gracefully, cat-like, her eyes narrowed, yet laughing.

'Wake up, my sweet. Didn't I make it clear that I'm feeling very lascivious, if that's the right word. Please, darling, can't we make a move upstairs?'

He forgot Sue; forgot his conscience; forgot everything but the violent temptation of his wife. Laughing, trembling, but suddenly full of strength, he picked her up in his arms and carried her up to bed.

14

For three days, Sue remained in the flat, smoking cigarettes, drinking endless cups of strong coffee but eating practically nothing. She did not answer the 'phone which rang several times. She wanted nothing more than to be left alone to nurse the dull aching pain in the pit of her stomach, and the bitterness in her mind and heart.

On the fourth day, Mary came round. One look at her sister's white, ravaged face; at the disordered flat, the unwashed dishes, and Mary *knew* the reason, even before Sue handed her Paul's letter.

Sue walked up and down, up and down, while Mary read. She kept rubbing her eyes. They were sore, red-rimmed. Her tongue felt dry and her limbs ached as though she had a fever. She braced herself for the sympathy Mary would show, afraid that the first kind word would penetrate the armour of pride which had so far kept her from breaking utterly. But Mary did not react quite as Sue expected. She quietly put Paul's letter down on the dusty coffee table in front of the sofa, took off her white beret and ran her fingers through her hair. Her lips were grim.

'Good. Now there's some hope for you, Sue!'

Sue looked down at the letter. She knew every word by heart. It was imprinted on her mind forever.

' . . . you must believe that I did love you, Sue, and I suppose I always will. By the time you get this, Melanie will have explained why you and I cannot go on living together and why a divorce is now out of the question.

Try not to think too badly of me, darling. When you get over the first disappointment, I am sure you will begin to realise that this is best for you as well as for me. I know my own weaknesses and I don't think I would have made you the right husband. I'm too used to the good things of life and I'm afraid I might have become very tiresome in the struggle to make ends meet. You would soon have stopped loving me and I'd rather we parted now when you still have, I hope, some good memories of the wonderful times we shared . . . Melanie understands me — better perhaps than I understand myself and . . . '

There was another page in the same vein but it wasn't really important. On that first page Paul had confirmed everything Melanie had said that morning when she called to see Sue.

'Paul is so weak and so hopelessly self-centred. He's never been poor you see, and never could bear to be. He'd make you utterly miserable and from all I hear you haven't a hard streak in your nature. I have, I admit it. I can cope with Paul. He is a taker, not a giver. If you really do love him, and I'm sure you must do after all this time, you'll see that you couldn't manage him. He'd let you down again and again, whenever it suited him. Take my advice and forget him. He isn't worth your kind of loving.'

Sue could agree now with everything Melanie — or Mary — had ever said about him. Paul was a worthless coward. He hadn't even had the courage to come and tell her himself that they were all washed up. For that alone, she would never forgive him. Yet it hadn't quite stopped her from loving him, wanting him, feeling that her life was shattered into so many pieces that she could never pick them up and re-make it.

'You're coming home with me now, this minute, Sue. Start packing. I've made up the bed in the spare room. I fancied something like this had happened when you didn't answer the 'phone. And don't argue with me. You're not staying here another minute. You look ghastly.'

Sue didn't care any more what happened. She felt too ill, too hurt. The lack of food and sleep had taken their toll, and she was on the point of collapse.

'Sleep is what you need,' Mary went on, 'Come along. We'll pack your things.'

When they finally reached the flat, Mary switched on the electric blanket in the spare-room and undressed Sue and got her to bed. The girl didn't seem to be able to stop shivering. A little while later, Mary's doctor came and gave Sue a quick examination and two sleeping pills. Mary heated up some thick chicken soup and made her take a few spoonfuls; then Sue slept. When she woke, twenty-four hours later, the full agony of what had happened hit her. Then she couldn't stop crying.

Mary remained calm and eminently helpful — more tactful than she had ever been before and more sympathetic.

Sue's anguish broke through even her composure. 'Get it over and done with,' she said, and her own eyes were wet.

'Then you can start forgetting the man. But don't you ever forget what he's done to you.'

'For nearly eight years I've loved him. I can't start hating him now!' Sue cried.

The memory of that half-hour with Paul's wife began to return and taunt her. She'd never met Melanie before; she'd always been a 'name' — a rather indistinct woman in a photograph that Paul had once shown her. Now she had become a person — a real living, breathing woman to whom Paul was married, and who he had said he didn't love. Was it all a lie? *Did* he love her? She was very very attractive. Sue had been unable to stop staring at that strangely beautiful yet hard face, the exquisite figure. But Sue curiously enough remembered Melanie without jealousy. Melanie wasn't really important. Only Paul mattered and the inhuman way in which he had broken all his promises and left her.

She got better physically and helped Mary in the flat. Joe was kin. They were both kind.

Huge bunches of flowers began to arrive regularly from Ross. Sue couldn't bear to look at them. Such attentions only served to highlight Paul's neglect.

'Why won't you see Ross?' Mary kept asking.

'Because I don't want to,' was Sue's reply.

Surely Mary ought to realise that of all the people in the world, Ross least of all, was welcome. She could not bear the thought of his love and pity. It struck at what remnants of pride she had left.

At the end of the week, Mary said:

'I think you *ought* to see poor old Ross, Sue. He's been so good to you and he's going away — abroad somewhere. You ought at least to thank him in person for his kindness and devotion. Do you know he brings those flowers himself, and telephones me twice a day to ask after you?'

At last Sue gave in. If Ross was leaving the country, maybe it was best that she should see him; make him understand that whilst she was grateful for all he had done, she did not want his love. She did not want any man, ever again.

Ross came into Mary's sitting-room looking somehow far larger, more solid, than she remembered. Sue could not find words to cover her sudden embarrassment. He seemed to have such timidity. He came over and kissed her gently on both cheeks.

'Thanks for seeing me. Mary said you were better, and I'd hoped to find you looking better. You're very pale and dreadfully thin, Sue.'

She'd forgotten the gentleness of that voice.

'Don't be sorry for me,' she said, her own voice rough as she turned away from him.

'Thank you for all the lovely flowers,' she

added, 'It was kind of you!'

He did not reply. When she turned her head to see if he had heard her, he was staring at her.

'I'd forgotten how lovely you are!' he said under his breath.

'Oh, Ross!' Tears suddenly pricked her eyelids. She swallowed, fought against the desire to weep and felt the hot tears running down her cheeks.

He came to her then and wiped the tears away with a large white handkerchief. Then he wrapped his arms about her, holding her tightly.

'Don't!' he said huskily, 'You know I can't bear to see you cry. I love you so much, Sue.'

She fought now not against her grief but against the comfort and security of his arms and his words.

'Let me go,' she whispered and tried to draw away from him. But he held her against him. 'Please, Ross — don't you see that this is not the way? I know you love me, but you've got to understand — *I'm still in love with Paul.*'

'Yes, I know!'

She looked up at him in surprise. Suddenly she saw that he was smiling down at her. 'That's not new news. Ever since the first day I met you, I've known you were in love with him. It doesn't alter anything. I still want you to marry me.'

'Ross!' Her voice sounded shocked and this time she did succeed in moving away from him. 'You know I can't do that. I don't love you. And I don't want to marry anyone, now — ever.'

'I'm going away,' Ross said, as though he hadn't heard her. 'To Australia, on business. I'll be gone a couple of months at least. I want you to come with me . . . as my wife. Sydney is the other side of the world, Sue. There's a new life waiting for us both there. Look . . . ' He took out his pocket book and laid two air tickets to Sydney on the table where she could see them. 'It's a deal worth several thousand pounds to my firm — perhaps even a quarter of a million. I don't want to lose it but I'm just not going without you. Understand? I'm going to blackmail you into coming with me, my darling.'

This statement seemed incredible, yet curiously enough she did not doubt that Ross meant every word he said.

She shook her head. She felt deeply distressed.

'Please, don't say any more. You must know I can't marry you. It would never work. I've been too long with Paul — eight years, Ross. That's nearly all my youth, isn't it? I've never loved anyone but Paul and I never will. If I married you, I'd have nothing to give you — nothing!'

For a moment, silence hung between them, then Ross said more to himself than to her:

'You once gave me the most wonderful night of my life. You didn't love me then and yet you gave me love as no other woman ever has. I want no other woman but you now. Don't you think I've tried to forget you? Tried, and failed. I'm the wrong end of thirty, Sue — old enough to know what I want; old cnough to have got myself a wife years ago if I'd found the woman I wanted. I waited because something told me that one day I'd meet you. I know that we belong together. I know that even the differences in our backgrounds don't matter because my love for you is stronger than social conventions. I'm not asking for your love, Sue — only for your presence near me; your companionship; your conversation; your laughter and your tears. I want the right to take care of you.'

'Ross, I can't. I can't take all you offer and give nothing back. I'm not made that way.'

He was smiling again.

'I know. Don't you think I'm aware of that? I saw what happened to you in France. It was the same then, wasn't it? You thought you had nothing to give, yet despite everything, you gave me your friendship and your body, too. You forgot Paul then, didn't you? *Admit* that he never came between us — not that last night . . .'

She bit her lip, confused by his arguments.

'You're talking of sex, not love!' she said harshly.

'Okay, I'm talking of sex. In that way, too, we belong. But there was more than bodily hunger between us and you know it. Appetites can be assuaged without tenderness or love. I'm not a romantic fool. I know it, Sue. There have been too many empty meaningless, loveless episodes in my past — nights that left a feeling of disgust next day and nothing but a wish never to have to see that other person again. But you can't convince me that only sex prompted your behaviour that night.'

She was silent, unable to argue with him now. He had brought back all too clearly the memory of those long hours in his arms — the wild sweet, unexpected joy of it. She had not thought of Paul — nor wanted to think of him then. But surely Ross must see that here lay the greatest danger — she could perhaps make use of him and let him help her to forget Paul. But if she allowed herself to do so, she would eventually despise herself — and him.

'Why?' Ross asked brutally as she tried to explain. 'If I can help you to put Paul out of your life, your heart will soon be free of him. Why should you hate me for that? Or yourself? Or do you want to live on sentimental memories, growing older and more bitter and more lonely as the wasted years go by? What a bloody waste! Or is it that you just can't stand the idea of being married to a common chap like me?'

Quickly, she covered his hand with her own. She had forgotten how sensitive he was about his background.

'Of course not. It isn't that. You know it isn't. It's just that you are asking the impossible, Ross. I'm not a whole person any more. I can't love — not just you, but anyone. I don't want to love anyone ever again. I don't *trust* love. I'll never trust another man as long as I live.'

Ross shook his head.

'No, Sue. Even now when you choose to think of yourself as empty and useless, you are giving me your consideration. You would come with me to Australia if you were thinking only of yourself. You're refusing because you are afraid for me. Is this the conduct of a bitter, hard girl who hates all men? If you hate me why bother about me? Why not 'use' me, as you put it? Just take what I offer?'

'No, because . . . ' she broke off, started again, 'because . . . oh, Ross, not *you* . . . you've been so good to me. I couldn't hurt *you*.'

'So you do care — however little, *you care*!' he cried triumphantly. 'I think I knew it in France and I know it now.'

'Perhaps, in time . . . maybe when you come back from Australia . . . ' she began hesitantly. But he broke in:

'No! I'm taking you with me, Sue — as my wife. You shall have time then . . . all the time you want. Time to learn to trust me; time to forget Paul and the past; time to learn to love me. I'm not going without you.'

'Ross, I can't, *I can't* come with you. I love Paul!'

'Do you?' His voice was suddenly hard and cynical. 'Do you? Or is he just a habit? The strongest habits can be broken, Sue, with a little will power. Do you *want* to go on loving him? Is he really worth it? I don't think so, and deep down in your heart, I don't believe you think so either. Your splendid lover had feet of clay and you who profess the need for honesty have to admit this.'

She covered her face with her hands.

'I know, but I still love him, despite everything. I do, Ross. I can't help it!'

'Yes, you can!'

Ross put his arms round her and bending his head, his mouth came down and took hers in a strange long kiss. There was passion, desire and even violence but it was controlled to a poignant tenderness that brought the swift colour to her cheeks and warmth to her frozen heart. Involuntarily, she struggled against him but he would not let her go. She felt her senses weakening — responding — and knew that her arms were fastening round his neck and that she was returning his kiss. She did not want to be physically aware of him; yet her body betrayed her. At last she wrenched her mouth away from his and gasped:

'This is only sex ... I don't want it ... I ... '

But his mouth came down on her again, silencing her, still with that same strangely insistent but controlled violence. She could feel his large strong hands heavy on her hips; knew that she enjoyed his touch, needed it; knew that if she stayed close to him a moment longer, this need would be as overwhelming as his for her. Then he released her, holding her still, but away from him, his eyes searching hers.

'I love you!' he said. 'I love you enough not to cheat. I could win you ... this way. I could make you need me the way Paul once made you need him. That was sex, Sue . . . the way he did it. But I won't cheat you as he did. I will win you this way.'

He drew her slowly to him again and rested his cheek against her hair. His hands cupped her face and his lips touched hers so softly that she barely felt their caress. Her body trembled, awakened to her innermost need for him — a need that was beginning now to release the tight band of pain round her heart; to penetrate her very thoughts until, unaware, her hand reached out to touch his hand; to stroke his thick crisp hair.

'I don't love you!' she heard her own voice full of sadness, of intolerable pain.

'I know!'

His answer hung between them, trembling in the silence as their bodies trembled.

'I may never be able to love you, Ross.'

'I know!' he said again.

'And you still want me?'

'Yes, I still want you.'

He met her eyes and smiled. 'I'll take the agony along with the ecstasy, my darling, if that's the way it has to be. I believe in love — in its power and its glory, as well as its pain. I believe that if you can trust me now, in time you may even grow to need me as much as I need you.'

'If I could believe that . . . '

'You don't have to believe it, Sue — only to give me your trust and faith. That is all.'

'I don't love you!' she said again.

'But I love you and that is all you need to know.'

'I do believe that. But I'm afraid, Ross.'

Gently, he took both her hands in his. The dry warmth of his palms closed over her cold fingers. Gradually this warmth passed to her. Perhaps he meant no more than the simple act of transmitting the healing electric current, and yet, in her new awareness, his action seemed symbolic. He was offering her the warmth of his life; showing her that though she had lost faith in men and in the world, he could restore both to her. He was promising that through him she could learn to love and to believe again.

'Will you come with me, Sue?' he asked.

She nodded her head. And left her hands in his, holding tight to the future and closing her tear-filled eyes on the past and its pain.

We do hope that you have enjoyed reading this large print book.

Did you know that all of our titles are available for purchase?

We publish a wide range of high quality large print books including:
Romances, Mysteries, Classics, General Fiction, Non Fiction and Westerns.

Special interest titles available in large print are:
The Little Oxford Dictionary
Music Book
Song Book
Hymn Book
Service Book

Also available from us courtesy of Oxford University Press:
Young Readers' Dictionary
(large print edition)
Young Readers' Thesaurus
(large print edition)

For further information or a free brochure, please contact us at:
Ulverscroft Large Print Books Ltd.,
The Green, Bradgate Road, Anstey,
Leicester, LE7 7FU, England.
Tel: (00 44) 0116 236 4325
Fax: (00 44) 0116 234 0205